TERROR RED

TERROR RED

COLONEL DAVID HUNT AND
CHRISTINE HUNSINGER

A TOM DOHERTY ASSOCIATES BOOK

NEW YORK

TERROR RED

Copyright © 2013 by David Hunt and Christine Hunsinger

Design by Mary A. Wirth

A Forge Book
Published by Tom Doherty Associates, LLC
175 Fifth Avenue
New York, NY 10010

www.tor-forge.com

Forge® is a registered trademark of Tom Doherty Associates, LLC.

Library of Congress Cataloging-in-Publication Data

Hunt, David.
   Terror Red / Colonel David Hunt and Christine
Hunsinger.—First edition.
        p. cm.
   "A Tom Doherty Associates book."
   ISBN 978-0-7653-3289-9 (hardcover)
   ISBN 978-1-4299-6540-8 (e-book)
   1. Terrorism—Prevention—Fiction.   2. Suspense fiction.
I. Hunsinger, Christine.   II. Title.
   PS3608.U5726T47 2013
   813'.6—dc23

                                        2012043278

Forge books may be purchased for educational, business, or promotional use. For information on bulk purchases, please contact Macmillan Corporate and Premium Sales Department at 1-800-221-7945 extension 5442 or write specialmarkets@macmillan.com.

First Edition: April 2013

Printed in the United States of America

0 9 8 7 6 5 4 3 2 1

To all those serving our nation, this book is dedicated to you.
—Colonel David Hunt

*For my mother, Kathie, and my children,
Jacob, Zachary and Kaileigh*
—Christine Hunsinger

ACKNOWLEDGMENTS

The good things about this book are a product of two writers trying to get it right. The coauthor Chris Hunsinger is a talented writer without whom this book would not have been written. Editing is the most difficult part of writing for me. Without the precise and accurate editing and advice from Susan North Mitchell, this book would have taken a less successful path. Howie Carr is the friend every book needs. Howie, thank you for introducing this book to Bob Gleason at Tor/Forge, Macmillan. Bob, without all your thoughtful editing and friendship this book would be less than it is. As always, my family's continued support was crucial, thank you all. Roger Ailes, the president of Fox News, continues to allow me on his network, which helps give this book a platform.

— DAVID HUNT

Special thanks to my mother, Kathie Hackett, who taught me to love books; to Michael, who made me want to write one; to Rick, who believed that I could; to my Aunt Pat, who kept the thought alive by constantly saying, "Someone in this family ought to write a book"; to my children, Jacob, Zachary and Kaileigh, for allowing me the time to write this and for occasionally thinking their mom is pretty cool; to Christian, for pulling me over the finish line; and to Kevin, for being in my day and for not letting my Rhode Island get in my way. Also, thanks to Governor Lincoln Chafee and the rest of my work family for guiding me through the crazy world of Rhode Island government. Most of all, thanks to David Hunt for his friendship, time and this opportunity.

— CHRISTINE HUNSINGER

SECTION I

*Happiness is having a large, loving, caring,
close-knit family in another city.*

—George Burns

I

New England Christmases are picture-postcard perfect, full of glittering, sparkling, twinkling everything. On December 26, everything turns gray: sky, snow, ice, moods, people; everything is Soviet-Union-stand-in-a-breadline gray. The shift is sudden, jarring and depressing. Brains hibernate, bodies autopilot and the countdown to St. Patrick's Day begins.

Today is December 26.

"I don't understand how you can work for that guy. He's completely sold out, you know. He's turned his back on everything the Democratic Party stands for. He's such a *politician,*" my sister whined.

I fiddled with the dial on the heater, hoping in vain that switching it on, off and on again would turn the slightly warm breeze to tropical wind. Freezing my butt off driving my sister to Logan was not my favorite hobby.

"I'm a political consultant. I work for politicians."

Three years ago, I was working for the Democratic Party in Pennsylvania. I was splitting my time between two campaigns, and it looked like we might actually win both. And then the crazy started. One of my guys threatened to kill his opponent in a televised debate on gun control and was arrested. Two days later, my other guy showed up at a fund-raiser dressed as Elvis. Apparently he had gone off his meds and was hearing voices. A week after those charmingly eccentric incidents, I packed everything I owned into giant, lawn-sized Hefty bags, threw them in the back of my car and left town.

Christina Marchetti, political consultant to the hapless and troubled, as well as the queen of running away.

I gritted my teeth and laid on the horn. Traffic was crawling toward the airport. Five minutes ago it had been swerving wildly at unsafe speeds. Given Boston drivers, in another five minutes we might all be driving sideways. With any luck, we would arrive at Logan before I bludgeoned my sister with an ice scraper. I was on vacation until New Year's Day, and although part of my job was to worry about the fate of the Democratic Party and its agenda, I figured it could wait a few days. Right now all I wanted to do was get my sister on her plane, go home to my apartment and slip into a coma.

From the bottom of my pocketbook came the muted theme music from the TV show *The West Wing*. That was how my phone rang when it worked. Yes, I was officially a dork.

I rooted around and found it, hit the button and said hello.

"Hi."

It was the singsongy voice of Mary Katherine. Mary Katherine Connolly was typical South Boston: 100 percent Irish, devoutly Catholic, pretty face and amazingly competent. She is Senator Kerrigan's constituent service coordinator because she speaks the language of the district's natives; also because she's from a political family and knows where all the bodies are buried. She basically runs every other department and function of Kerrigan's office. Make no mistake. She's in charge.

"Hey, what's up?" I said with a pout.

"I can hear that you are still in your Happy Christmas mood, so I will make this short. Received another update on the terror alert. It's gone up again, but I can't really quantify how. Since we did away with the color coding it all seems very vague to me, but I thought I should call you. There is extra emphasis on this one because President Carson is spending the holidays in Maine with the Wheeler family."

The terror alert rose and fell three times a day. When I started working for Kerrigan, I cared. Now I ignored it. After all this time, with nothing happening, I embraced the myth that we were safe.

"Okay, so we're at persimmon? Or is it magenta? Go ahead and let the senator know."

Kate laughed and we disconnected.

Colleen picked up right where she'd left off.

"He'll never be President. My generation expects a lot more than Senator Brian Kerrigan has to offer."

Groan.

Brian Kerrigan was the sanest politician I'd worked for, and while that wasn't saying a whole lot, I'd take it.

After the Pennsylvania debacle, twenty-six years old, spectacularly humiliated, close to broke and with limited options—my car had autopiloted its way in the direction of home. The eight-hour drive north had been just long enough for my brain to convince itself that the bizarre and embarrassing moments that make up my life would somehow be easier to deal with if I lived closer to my family.

My family *is* bizarre and embarrassing, in a lovable sort of way; we make a sport out of driving each other insane. We're loud and messy, but the truth of it is we'd be lost without each other.

Eventually I'd wound up living in Boston, one whole, if rather small, state away from my family. Part of my mental calculus definitely included that if I lived in Providence, every time I ran to the store in sweatpants and a ratty old T-shirt some relative would call my mother and tell her I wasn't dressed appropriately.

I didn't have any relatives in Boston, so way fewer tattling phone calls were bound to happen; distance was a good thing, in that absence makes the heart grow fonder; I could see them on my terms; and I was way less likely to discover that the cute guy I was talking to in a bar was a second cousin. It was a good plan, but there were flaws.

My sister Colleen had moved to Washington, D.C., but in typical New Englander fashion continuously found reasons to fly back home. Flights to Boston's Logan Airport were cheaper than those to Providence. Naturally, it became my job to pick her up and get her back to Rhode Island.

I could hear the evil little karma trolls laughing.

Snow and rain blowing sideways, ugly gray sky, no clouds, no sun, nasty New England day. We are driving down Route 128 southbound, eighteen miles from Logan Airport just outside of Boston, a poorly designed, always jammed piece of asphalt that is the lifeblood of the southern part of Massachusetts. Wicked cold, a few people walking around and those brave souls are bundled up to their ears. Cars sliding all over the road, what the hell are you doing out in this type of weather kind of day? My bet is that God saves the good weather for Christmas Day, then gets pissed off and gives us a day like this.

A Ford Escort just came up on my tail and wanted into the backseat. Then he passed me in the breakdown lane. The breakdown lane in a Ford Escort, for Christ's sake? If I were not carrying such valuable cargo, I would demonstrate for him just exactly how to drive. My vehicle is an oversized, powerful Cadillac Escalade with twenty-two-inch tires and a few other tricks up its shiny black sleeves. It's a thing of beauty. The only thing missing on this car is a ram, and at these speeds I may not need that. We in the car are safe, but the rest of the population had better think twice.

My cargo is the best damn woman in the whole world, my mother. For the first time since my father's death last year, she's finally cutting loose; which to her means going farther from the house than the local supermarket. Dad's death took a part of all of us with him. I bet it is harder for Ma than for me.

But she is dealing with it, and this trip to D.C. with her friend Martha is a great start.

"David, you know your aggressive driving bothers me, son. What happens if a deer comes running out, or a bear, or squirrel, or a bird flies straight at us?"

I want to say, *I will kill them; it is what I was trained to do, have done and will do again. I have been to a dozen driving schools and been in enough firefights in and around roads with things blowing up that this little excursion is simply not a problem.*

But instead I say, "Ma, I got this. Please trust me, and I love you."

"If you are so smart, wired and connected, how come you didn't know where bin Laden was hiding?" chirps my wicked, sarcastic mom.

"Who do you think told SEAL Team Six?" I say with a smirk.

Multiple pieces of popcorn come flying from the backseat, one even hitting me in the head. They are eating popcorn in my car? They must have packed snacks for the plane ride. Airport security is going to love that.

"You two lovelies will pick up all the kernels in the backseat before you leave." Usually I don't allow food in the car, but since it's Mom and Martha, okay.

The banter is cut short by a call coming in on my Bluetooth. It's an unknown number, which means either the government or one of the boys is calling. I tap the screen on my Kensington 1600 system.

"Dave Gibson speaking."

"Gibster, Kor Dog here. Where are you now?"

"Tony, how are you? I am south of Boston."

Tony is a contract officer with the CIA. Tony and I have worked together, officially, a couple of times. He loves to call and update me just to see if my information is as current as his. Most of the time it's as good; sometimes it's better.

"Look, the terrorist chatter is getting very loud. We keep hearing about the East Coast. Why the hell would they still care about the East Coast, Colonel?"

"You mean besides Boston, New York City, Philadelphia and D.C.? Tony, you are losing it. I've got my own problems. It's the day after Christmas, I'm retired and I'm driving my mother to the airport. Let me know when it's more than chatter. Thanks for the call."

Since 9/11, this business of interpreting terrorism chatter has become a growth industry. More often than not, everyone's guessing, and there seems to be another looming crisis every week. I'm glad he called, but there is no *there* there, yet.

I know the world has its problems, but right now I've got my own. I'm really not looking forward to this. I hate airports. They're messy and crowded; half the people are depressed because they're being left behind by someone, and the other half are close to certifiable because their best something—girl, guy, whatever—is coming off the plane and who knows how things have changed since they've been gone. I gained this insight in the service of our country, in the United States Army Special Forces flying in back or on the floor of transport planes for more years than I can count. Colonel David Gibson, technically retired.

Another reason I hate airports is that, for some stupid reason, they always make me think of my father.

My father, who besides being a genuine hero of World War II, having the brain of a genius and being an Olympic-caliber swimmer, was also the best man I ever met—period. But he could be more than painful about things like getting to an airport on time. He gave me enormous love and support in whatever I did, and I miss him every day. Lately I sometimes feel lost without him. I am probably a bit too old to be that way . . . but there is just something about fathers and sons.

Took me years to realize that there was a one-sided competition going on and that I was trying to be a better man than my father. Hell, I was trying to be better at anything than he was. I may have been a better officer in the Army, but he had World War II and I had Afghanistan, Iraq and Bosnia, all in and out of uniform. His was a war we won that they made movies about; mine just lasted too damn long for anyone to care.

I usually manage to avoid the airport thing, but for Mom, anything. She has lost her husband and two sons. It's just me and my sister left, so I will stand in a bucket of cold water in front of the United Airlines ticket counter if it will help my mother.

The car in front of me taps the brakes and slides to the left. Cold-ass December with a little snow falling only makes bad drivers worse. Now we stop while the idiot in front tries to get his vehicle back to straight as opposed to sliding.

I hate traffic. I hate all forms of traffic. Traffic is a line, and after twenty-nine years in the military I have a strong aversion to and a deep hatred for lines. Hence, hating traffic is unavoidable. Boston traffic is so bad it should be illegal.

Mom and Martha are nattering nonstop in the backseat, the radio is playing Bob Seger which makes me want to drive fast but I'm trapped in traffic on my way to the airport.

Happy holidays. You have got to be kidding me!

3

Colleen was going on and on, traffic was still sitting still and I was making a list of creative ways to kill myself.

1. Freeze to death in snowbank.
2. Leap from moving vehicle—except the car wasn't moving.
3. Spontaneously combust.

The list was originally supposed to be all of the things I'd rather do with the hour and a half of my life that this trip was devouring, but the list took a nasty turn south when Colleen launched into a cataloguing of the psychological ramifications of being related to me and the rest of our family.

For Christmas I had given Colleen a sweater. She'd given me a book called *Finding Yourself: A Guide*. I'd never had finding-myself issues. If I needed to find myself, I looked down. I was usually there.

This last week she must have tried to engage me in the how-it-sucks-that-we-don't-have-a-real-family-anymore conversation about a hundred times and kept repeating, "It's such a shock to find out your whole life is a lie."

Mutter, eye roll, big sigh: Come on! Get over it already; it'd been ten years since our parents divorced.

Colleen is four years younger than me. She's five-foot-five and what she calls voluptuous. She's trendy and chic and her clothes only cover half her body, half the time. I'm six feet tall, skinny as a rail and not even the eighty-five-dollar bra from Victoria's Secret can get me close to voluptuous. She's dark-haired and olive-skinned, "Just like Sophia Loren," says my Italian father. If Sophia Loren had a butt the size of Cleveland—but no, I'm not bitter. My red hair and pale complexion come from my mother and make up the Irish side of the genetic coin. Colleen and I are both difficult and argumentative and will fight to the death for the last word.

Recently, my mother had given me a lecture on the finer points of sisterhood and guilted me into the trying-not-to's: trying not to argue with Colleen, trying not to get angry with Colleen, trying not to comment on the size of Colleen's ass. Today it was causing me physical pain. Colleen had been a philosophy major in college, which she figured entitled her to share her opinion on everything. Trouble was, Colleen was convinced her opinion was the only opinion and she'd argue with you until you either gave in and agreed with her or attempted suicide with the closest implement that would open a vein.

I was about to rummage around in my pocketbook for a nail file when we reached the end of the Ted Williams Tunnel and traffic magically cleared. Five minutes later, we pulled into the parking area of Logan Airport. In ten more minutes she'd be on a plane and I'd be back in my car and on my way home, free to enjoy the rest of my vacation.

"David, what is it exactly that you do?"

Ever since I've retired, Martha has developed a fascination with my work. She's taken up reading spy novels and such and asking me bizarre questions. Last week she wanted to know if it was really possible to kill a person with a pencil eraser.

"Your mother and I were wondering what to tell people when they ask."

"Oh, no, Martha. You leave me out of this," my mother says.

"Oh, hush. David, we know you did do some rather seedy things in the military, but what exactly do you do now? Is it the Masked Marvel comic book idea you had when you were twelve, or is it more the Mad-Mercenary-laying-waste-of-African-villages type of work that we have been reading about?"

I know I shouldn't, but I can't help myself.

"Martha," I say in a very serious voice, "I live in a very dark cave and only come out when it's time to feed. If I tell you any more than that, I will have to kill you."

Actually, I just finished a job in South Africa, and it didn't involve erasers or caves. The South Africans have some great special forces and a world-class intelligence service. It was a real pleasure doing executive protection contracts for a handful of European fat cats on holiday. I will use some of the South Africans on my next job coming up in Belgium. The job is boring but the boys will make it fun.

Sometimes I get to do some work for Uncle Sam; usually

it's just looking someone up or checking on something for the FBI or CIA. This time I spent a few days checking out recent bombings as a favor to our embassy, while in Cape Town doing some executive protection for a European firm.

Last year at this time, just before I retired, I was running around the mountains and setting up operations with the boys from Langley and our special operations forces. It was a hell of a way to end a career. We did good.

I really miss it. I miss the soldiers; how they laughed, cried and loved to hate most of us in the officer corps. I miss the things we did together, the impossible tasks solved in the middle of the night. I miss the women I loved and left—who probably only loved me because I was leaving.

I don't miss the endless meetings, nor the poor pay, nor the times of senseless killing. Most of all, I do not miss the incompetence of some of those who presumed to lead without the slightest idea of what that meant. They were supposed to be leading soldiers into battle when instead they were promoting themselves and playing politics.

I concentrate on the radio to drown out the nattering in the backseat. The news break at the top of the hour announces that government sources are reporting a large amount of intelligence chatter concerning the Muslim Brotherhood. The government is considering raising the terror alert status. Nothing more specific, so I know more than they do. Raising the alert status is just plain silly; the whole alert thing is a joke anyway. But after hearing from Tony, I'm wondering if this is more than just the standard crisis of the week.

"David, isn't that our exit?" asks Ma.

She's right. It is.

I move the 2008 black and beautiful Cadillac Escalade through the tunnel and park. As I open the door, cold, damp wind from Boston Harbor makes me pull my coat on tighter, and I tell my passengers, "Button up, ladies, it's cold and nasty out here." I get the bags out for Mom and Martha. Damn, but she is looking good in the brown beaver full-length coat and hat I gave her for Christmas. Knock 'em dead, Ma.

"Damn it, Mom. You are only going to D.C. for five days and this bag weighs more than the two of you put together."

She and Martha start talking about how many magazines they each brought, how many games of Sudoku they would play and whether or not they had their mall sneakers with them. I tune out. I've heard this before. They carry small bags for everything, bags to carry bags, bags in case they go shopping, bags to hide things . . . this is only one of the many things I don't get about women.

Logan Airport is backed up to Boston Harbor by some undesirable parts of East Boston and a tangle of highways and tunnels. Bound by water on three sides, it's had no place to expand over the years, and the use of airplanes has increased slightly since Logan was built in the early 1920s. So it's been built up, gotten denser, used every square foot of dry land it can find. It's the physical size of a small city's airport, but with the traffic and international flights of a major destination. Clustered, confusing and rarely quiet, very little of Logan is wasted on "beautification." It's too busy working.

The airport is crowded and messy and the air is full of anxiety. Logan Airport may have been pretty once, just not in my lifetime. Dirty concrete walls, floors of old worn-out rugs and linoleum, tall support posts and windows with no real view. The ticket counters with people on both sides not wanting to be there. The building and the people just look tired. I herd my mother and Martha to the check-in counter. They look scared. I give them credit for trying new things at their age.

Then Martha almost blows it.

"Marge, I don't think we should go. I don't think it's safe."

"Martha, don't start with that again."

"Mom, Martha, you are both going to have a great time. Just relax. There is nothing to be scared about. We are now in an airport that is safer than it's ever been. As long as I am here, you are safe. And when you leave my side, I will extend the famous Colonel Gibson protection bubble over you both. Now please relax. You'll be fine."

"David, you promise me that I will be okay," Martha demands.

"Damn, of course not, Martha. You will be the only one in trouble on that entire plane."

Martha is calmer now, but it could still go either way. My mom changes the subject to something both women can get behind.

"David, do you have plans for New Year's?"

I know where this is going. I ignore her.

My mom and Martha are ready to make their way through the metal detectors and be off. I am ready to get the hell out of here.

"You two lovely young women are all set. Have fun in our nation's capital and stay away from biker bars."

Martha looks skeptical.

I hold up my hand and say, "All you have to do is get on that shiny cigar-shaped instrument. Now, please, enough of this. Get going."

I hug them both and they finally confront their fears and move to the security gates for their flight.

As I move through the crowd, my phone chirps. When I check, there is a message waiting. Must have missed it in the tunnel or in the parking garage.

"David, Tony here. Much of the 'chatter' we're hearing is about the Muslim Brotherhood, the Northeast and the time frame is this week."

Okay, so that is a little more specific. Probably nothing to get excited about, but I should hang around until Mom's plane is in the air.

5

I had my head down against the wind, was trudging through the gray slop that only yesterday had been magic Christmas snow, and my less-than-stellar mood tanked even more.

We blew through the door to the terminal on a gust of wind and stood there stamping our feet trying to ward off frostbite. The Calvin Klein cashmere coat my mother had bought me for Christmas was trendy and chic and a pointed message that I needed to start wearing grown-up clothes. What it wasn't was hike-through-the-tundra-approved. Neither were the chunky-heeled, funky boots that came with the coat. I was just now discovering that they weren't waterproof, but on the positive side, they were giving me blisters.

Why didn't I just drop her at the door and drive off?

We did the airport shuffle: checking bags, locating IDs, losing IDs and finding them again. At the security checkpoint we started the good-byes and then did a whole other thing instead.

"You have to come and visit. We'll go out. I know all the cool places in D.C. now. There are some majorly hot guys who would just die if I set them up with you."

Yeah, that was just what I needed.

Actually, it probably was, but I had given up men for Lent last year and was not looking to change that. While my permanently single status presented certain issues regarding what to do on Friday nights, which cousin or gay friend to bribe into escorting me to weddings and which chick flick to rent for New Year's Eve, I mostly liked being alone.

"It's been a year since you and Mac broke up."

Of course Colleen would choose this moment to probe gently at my psyche with a sledgehammer. My right eye began to twitch. Eighty-one days until St. Patrick's Day.

Jack McKenna was a Boston city cop. We'd met at a fund-raiser for the newly elected Boston mayor, where one too many glasses of wine, Mac's crooked grin and his quick wit charmed and captivated me. Against all my better judgment and all the strict rules I'd had against dating men whose professions included a high probability of death—cops, firemen, military guys, armed robbers—we became a thing.

Mac was all guy, all in charge, all the time. It was one of those whirlwind things where you couldn't catch your breath and often couldn't find your pants and it was over as quickly as it had begun.

The throbbing started behind my left eye, a sure sign that a migraine was on its way.

Colleen and I did finally hug and say good-bye and I promised to find time to visit. It was just a small lie, the kind that kept us from arguing and me from throttling her right here in the airport. It was the good kind.

Exhaustion, a headache from hell and the thought of walking the nine thousand miles back to my car made me turn left instead of right. I needed pie.

6

GIBSON

I noticed a familiar face next to the information booth at Terminal B on my way in. His name is Peter-something. The last name will come to me, or I'll get it as I get closer and can read his name tag.

The last time I saw Pete, he was trying not to look scared while rappelling down the side of a building. I was looking down at him. That's what rappelling instructors do . . . look down on their students and tell them that no matter what they think, they are not going to die.

Pete is now a trooper with the Massachusetts State Police, working the holidays and looking pretty bored. He doesn't see me approach the booth. I get right up next to his gun hand, just in case he gets nervous.

"So, Trooper Johnson, you stopped wetting your pants over heights yet?"

The quiet, menacing tone of my voice makes him try to step away as he turns to face me. His face registers recognition and relaxes.

"Colonel Gibson. Sir, how are you?" The rest of it sounds like blah, blah, blah.

"Drop the bullshit, Pete. It's just me saying hi. So, hi and how the hell are you?"

We make it through the basics. I've recently retired from the Army and have my own private security company. Pete Johnson is married, three kids, house in Revere. Things are good.

Pete's radio squawks; some kind of problem on the runway. Then an announcement is made in a deafening volume over the loudspeaker. The airport is being shut down. No one is to leave. Seconds after the radio call, televisions all over the airport flash news alerts and special reports. Fox News has live pictures of the flight I just put my mother on. It is sitting at the end of the runway.

I beelined for the airport Cheers, which is modeled after the Hollywood version of Cheers, which looks nothing like the real pub located on Beacon Hill. TVs lined the wall, each one tuned to a different twenty-four-hour news station. People talked, bags rolled and banged, the automated no-smoking announcement went on at regular intervals. The sounds combined to form a wall of white noise that was oddly calming and successfully drowning out my crabby mood. Cup of coffee number two doused the headache, the pie and ice cream did away with the pit in my stomach and gradually my shoulders lowered from their holiday-induced, defensive, braced-for-drama position.

Hoping to catch the score of the Celtics game, I scanned the wall of televisions. My eyes focused on the Fox News Alert graphic sliding across one of the screens.

Probably another Los Angeles car chase they'd broadcast for six hours until the idiot running from the cops ran out of gas or plunged into a crowd, killing a family of four. My weakness, when it came to TV, was that I would sit for hours in front of it afraid that if I turned it off I'd miss something important. I fought the urge to get sucked into ridiculousness and lost.

The Fox News Alert graphic was still there, but now there was a caption that read *LOGAN AIRPORT* and live footage of an airplane on the runway.

The work part of my brain kicked in. Kerrigan sat on the Joint Committee on Intelligence, and Massachusetts was his home state. No matter what this "incident" turned out to be, my vacation was on hold for the foreseeable future while we coordinated statements and drafted next steps.

"Hey! Turn that up," someone yelled from the other end of the counter.

A round and wrinkled waitress long past caring grabbed a remote and yelled back, "Keep your shorts on." The New England hospitality made me smile. I was fumbling through my purse looking for a pen and my BlackBerry when the sound came up.

". . . details are sketchy at this time, but sources are saying that US Airways Flight 1872 taxied to the end of the runway fifteen minutes ago and came to a stop. There has been no contact with the plane since. Authorities are not commenting on the situation so far, but there is some speculation, since the recent rise in terror alert status, that this will be treated like a . . ."

Terror alert. Flight 1872. Colleen's plane.

Crap.

I threw money on the counter and almost ran out of the bar.

I rounded the corner trying to find the information booth I'd noticed earlier and almost smacked into a crowd of people. Most of them looked scared, some were crying, others were yelling out questions to the two state police officers who were manning the booth.

Just then a healthy dose of denial showed up.

This is not happening. This is really not happening.

My eyes landed on the man at the front of the line. He looked to be early forties and was obviously military: all muscle, bone-straight posture and an air of being in control. He was leaning over the counter talking to the police, and the police were talking back, obviously exchanging information with him. In the midst of what looked like mass hysteria and pandemonium, he was calm.

GIBSON

Trooper Johnson is unimpressed. Since 9/11, this kind of stuff happens a lot. He starts telling me stories about all of the times they've done this and the ridiculous reasons for it. Johnson's probably right, this is almost certainly not a big deal, but Mom's on the plane and that makes me a little more interested.

While he's talking, it has taken three minutes for the airport to reach critical mass. Cell phones are going off, cops are coming from every direction, lines are forming everywhere. The frenzy feeds on itself and soon people are pushing and yelling and straining to hear the television reports. The news coverage focuses on the panic, since they obviously don't know anything about the plane.

Pete's radio squawks again. No new information is passed, but the tone of voice of the guy on the other end has a different quality. I am starting to get a bad feeling. I say good-bye to Pete and quickly walk away. I'm heading to the exit, the Black Beauty and my bag, to do what I do, when beautiful chaos comes careening out of the crowd and stops right in front of me. She has the most amazing green eyes.

She's attractive in an unforced sort of way, a little wild and a little anxious. There was something in her walk and her eyes that would not let me look away. She has to be six feet tall, which certainly adds to the first impression. She has trouble written all over her.

SECTION II

A particularly beautiful woman is a source of terror.
As a rule, a beautiful woman is a terrible disappointment.

—CARL JUNG

1

Creative cursing echoed behind me as I elbowed my way through the pissed-off New Englanders who took polite as a sign of weakness. Finally the crowd spit me out and I wobbled to a stop in front of Mr. Calm.

He actually looked half amused.

"Excuse me. Hi . . ." I stuck out my hand. "Christina Marchetti."

He didn't shake my hand, just stared at me with piercing blue eyes.

He was ruggedly handsome: broad shoulders, muscular but not steroid-using-freak muscular, dark hair with a hint of gray. He wore a bulky knit oatmeal sweater and toast-colored wool slacks with a black fleck. His loafers were perfectly polished.

"Sorry to bother you. I saw you talking to the police. I was wondering if you could tell me what's happening."

The voice that answered was deep and gravelly.

"It's either mechanical or a hijacking."

The word *hijacking* stopped my heart and caused me to break out in a cold sweat. Hysteria isn't something I'm comfortable with, so I swallowed hard and outwardly adopted matter-of-fact. I blinked twice and tried to appear calm.

"How about an educated guess as to which one is more likely?"

"What makes you think I would have a clue?"

Good question.

I shrugged. "Gut feeling? Woman's intuition? I'm not sure. You just look like you'd know these kinds of things."

"I think it's a hijacking."

Just then a voice came over the loudspeaker.

"Attention, ladies and gentlemen. The state police have requested that all persons having a connection to US Airways Flight 1872 please report to the US Airways check-in counter. Again, anyone having a connection to US Airways Flight 1872, please report to the US Airways check-in counter."

"It's a hijacking."

He turned and strode away. I stood there for a minute, stunned. Then I scrambled after him.

2

Pete runs after me, and of course the tall redhead is following. Christina-something, I think she said. Pete looks sort of sheepish when he tells me no one is leaving, including me. He says I will have to answer some administrative questions for the airline and, of course, some government officials; a euphemistic way of saying, *You are about to be screwed, blued and tattooed.*

"Will all waiting passengers or guests for US Airways Flight 1872 please move to Room 22 in Terminal B," says the rather officious-sounding voice.

So, okay. I give up. I'll go and do whatever, even though I am really against mass movements and cattle-herding. Stand here, go there. Did that for twenty-nine years, got the T-shirt and the hat. Besides, me trying to leave now and drawing unwanted attention to myself might cause me to be delayed even longer. Better to do what they ask for a while until I can figure out how to get to the people in charge and help Mom in my own way.

I hit the speed dial on my BlackBerry. "Tony, everything you know, now. My mother is on this plane."

"We got the Muslim Brotherhood, Colonel. No demands, and SFOD-D [Special Forces Operational Detachment-Delta] is on the way."

"Thanks, Tony. I am at the airport if you guys need anything."

"Good to know, Dave, thanks," and we both hang up.

I stood there too long trying to make the word *hijacking* mean something real and got caught up in the flow of people being herded into a room off the terminal. Mr. Calm melted into the crowd and disappeared.

Time flew by and stood still. No windows to see outside, no clocks on the walls and I didn't own a watch. Ten minutes or two hours? I couldn't tell. We had all been instructed to turn off our cell phones and I was lost without mine.

Work crises are things I live for and thrive on. Political malfunctions and media mishaps have a rhythm and cadence that drives actions, reactions, word choice, etc. . . . Simply everything you do in response is driven by the pulse of the story. If you do it well, you can wind up better-positioned than when you started. If you do it poorly, you wind up destroyed. Either way, the high you get while you're doing it is a slow, controlled burning stream of adrenaline. If you win, the rush comes at the end, usually in a burst of dancing on tables and wild animal sex on top of the office copier. If you lose, there's crushing depression and the filing of unemployment forms.

Personal crises, for me, are very different. They start out with a burst of adrenaline, followed by shaking and panic and then the bottom falls out of my stomach and usually I throw up.

Today, I was getting hit with a combination of personal and professional crises and, although I had so far avoided the throwing up part, my body responded with disbelief, numbness and enough panic to propel me into action without a plan. Never a good thing.

Fear raged in the personal half of my brain: sister, terrorists, death; my mother was going to kill me. Annoyance was rapidly climbing to uncontrolled anger in the work part. Without access to a clock and the Internet and TV and people feeding me information about what was going on, I couldn't do my job; I couldn't think about how to talk about what I didn't know.

The fidgeting came first, followed by the rifling through my purse looking for nothing, then the toe-tapping and finally the pacing. I briefly wandered around looking for Mr. Calm, but he was nowhere to be found. Some people have the ability to make themselves invisible in a room. It doesn't matter how big or loud they are in the outside world; when the need arises, they somehow fold in on themselves, stand still and disappear. It's an admirable and useful skill, and one that I don't have. I have a tendency to make a scene.

Just as I started lap three of the room, two no-neck policemen approached. Somewhere in the back of my head a voice whispered, *If you act crazy, people will think you are crazy.*

"Ma'am, could we please see some identification?" Crap.

Twelve one-dollar bills, my Senate ID, three pens and a tampon were fished out of my purse before I could locate my driver's license. I handed it over.

Officer 1 studied it; Officer 2 studied me. I glared, fidgeted, rifled, tapped my foot, paced and generally exhibited the exact behavior profile of someone who was involved in a hijacking.

We went through a list of questions. Why was I here? Who was I dropping off? What did my sister do for a living? Why was she going to D.C.? I answered them all, and then I answered them again. The third time around, my impatience took over and I was snide. The fourth time, the yelling began. Crazy, shrill girl yelling; probably some finger-pointing too.

I finished, folded my arms across my chest and stuck my chin out.

Officer 1 puffed up his chest and did the menacing cop stare. Officer 2 met my eyes and gave me a nasty little smile.

"Ma'am. Please step over here and empty the contents of your bag."

I didn't think they could search me or my bag, but since 9/11, authority and legal limitations were a bit fuzzy. The Patriot Act probably had some clause in it that read ". . . all women over five-foot-eleven will surrender all their rights."

Given the circumstances, now probably would have been the time to give in, let them look in my bag, take a seat and shut up. I almost never do what I'm supposed to do.

4

GIBSON

First she's being questioned by two state police who seem pretty impressed with themselves. Then she is having a piece of their asses. Trouble is, they like it. I should just get the hell out of here; but this is wrong on so many levels. I make a phone call because I know how the system here works.

My friend Duke and I have run three hijacking exercises here. We were helping the FBI and the city of Boston get ready for the qualifying rounds of the Summer Olympics soccer matches. As neither Duke nor I will take money from cops to help them, I have some huge IOUs. One of these favors is about to be called in with the commander of the Massachusetts State Police, Colonel Owen Jameson.

"Colonel Jameson, Dave Gibson. How are you, sir?"

I love calling this guy "sir." I need him right now.

"Sir, I am at the airport and I realize, considering what is going on, that this call is a bit out of order, but two of your guys are stepping way out of line with a woman who has her sister on the hijacked plane on your runway. I will need your help in about one minute."

After a brief conversation, I disconnect and head in their direction. I get close enough to hear the word "bitch" being used. That's enough.

I grab a coffee off the refreshment table US Airways has set up and keep moving.

"Oh, shit. I'm sorry."

Coffee goes everywhere. All over the table, all over one of

the policemen's shiny boots, all over his paperwork. He bends down to pick up the mess. My foot connects with the leg of the table, causing it to collapse. I'm all apologies and reach down to help. When he starts to rise, I grab two things—his balls and his gun holster. I put pressure on both and ease him down into a chair.

His partner is trying to decide which to go for, his weapon or his radio. Right now he doesn't know whether to shit or go blind. He knows what I just did and how fast I did it means he could be next.

His cell phone rings.

"Answer it," I say.

He has hesitated too long, and now his only option is to follow my directions.

I lean in, and in a low and calm voice say into Ball Boy's ear, "You have just violated four very serious rules of your own department. But what you really have to be concerned about right now is that I may be changing you from a buck to a doe."

The trooper with the phone is nodding and making movements with his mouth, but no sound is coming out.

"It's for you," comes out like a squeak as he holds the phone out to me.

I let go of Ball Boy and grab the phone.

Major Fuller, commander of F Troop at Logan Airport, is on the line.

"What the hell is going on? I understand two of my men are causing trouble with a woman. I don't have time for this, there is a problem on the runway."

"Major Fuller? Colonel Gibson. Nice to talk to you. Haven't seen you since we did the hijack training here last year. No problem here. Your men have conducted themselves with great distinction in this crisis. But I need to talk to you soon because my mother is on that plane."

I disconnect and toss back the cell phone.

No time for this. Hell is breaking loose and I need to get in the middle of it.

Three seconds later, in a blur of graceful and violent movement, it was over. Officer 1 and 2 stood overpowered, embarrassed and apologizing. Mr. Not-so-Calm had turned and was heading out the door. I grabbed my jaw off the floor and hurried after him, taking advantage of the moment to escape.

Relief, embarrassment and anger surged through me and made my hands shake. Mostly it was just redirected emotions and adrenaline from my earlier outburst, but enough of it was new. I had done a dumb ass thing, it had gone sideways, and badly, and someone I didn't know rescued me from my own stupidity. To top it off, he'd done it with a certain amount of macho, knight-of-the-Round-Table-violent flair.

Being rescued is something that happens in romance novels, westerns and occasionally an X-rated Indiana Jones fantasy. I really hate it when it happens to me.

"Hey!"

He turned around and was wearing the half smile I'd seen on him earlier.

"What the hell was that?"

"You're very welcome."

My blood pressure shot up.

"Excuse me? You're expecting me to thank you? Did I ask for your help? I was doing just fine."

"You were not doing just fine. You managed to have those cops so pissed off they were ready to have you declared an enemy combatant and drop you down a hole. This really isn't the time to be pissing off the police. Look, I admire your passion, but maybe you want to try thinking before you speak."

His expression was smug and condescending and dared me to disagree. The tirade was like being punched in the stomach, especially since thinking before I speak was one of my weaker areas.

"Whatever."

Whatever is my default term when I've been beaten in an argument or don't want to talk about something or when I feel outclassed or outgunned. I say *whatever* a lot, even though it's incredibly fourteen-year-old-girl and my experience is that it tends to annoy people.

Right now, annoying was just what I was shooting for.

" 'Whatever'?"

He paused and something—annoyance? incredulity?—slid across his face. "My mother is on that plane, and I need to see what I can do about that." He turned.

"Wait."

He turned back. "Look, who have you got on the plane?"

"My sister, Colleen."

"Your sister, my mother and one hundred and forty-six other passengers are on that plane; and I do not have the time to give you the short version of Terrorism 101. I have to go and help where I can. I have to get out of here before that becomes even more impossible than it already is."

The last part of it was said more to himself than to me, but it was the only thing that stuck: *Get out of here.* Getting out of here would be good.

He was moving toward a door marked PERSONNEL ONLY. I was tired of chasing after him and wasn't even sure why I was chasing after him, except he was the only one who seemed to be doing anything.

I wanted to do anything. I had to get him to take me with him, at least out of the airport.

"I might be able to help."

He laughed, but it was without any humor. It was snide and filled with doubt and a different kind of dare. I had to clench my fists to keep from taking a swing at him.

"What do you know that could possibly help me?"

I took a deep breath and tried to locate calm and a way in which I could help.

"I said I might be able to help. I work for Senator Kerrigan. He's a U.S. senator from Massachusetts and the ranking member of the Joint Committee on Intelligence. He'll be kept in the loop. That could help."

It didn't totally go unnoticed that I had just agreed to give fairly confidential information to someone I didn't know, but it was all I had.

I held my breath and waited out his silence.

"You really work for Kerrigan?"

"No, I was only kidding."

He narrowed his eyes at me and I stared back.

Finally he sighed and ran a hand over his face.

"I know you're going to be more trouble than you're worth, but come on."

He started down the stairwell. For a brief second I felt like I had won. Won what? I didn't know and it didn't matter, because the feeling was short-lived. At the bottom of the stairs, he turned and backed me into a corner. It took every ounce of courage I had to meet his eyes and not turn away.

"Here's the deal. You can't get to your car right now. This place is locked down. No public or private transportation is going in or out. There is the smallest of chances that your connection to Kerrigan will actually be of some help. So right now you can tag along.

"There are rules, and you will follow the rules. You will sit in the passenger seat. You will wear the seat belt. You will do what I say, when I say. I know what I'm doing. You do not."

He walked to the door and pushed it open. Subfreezing air blew in.

He looked over at me and said, "And you will not touch any of the dials in my car."

6

We reach the Escalade and I await the swoon. She apparently fails to recognize the glossy beauty before her, so after a sigh, I hit the unlock button and open the passenger door. She saunters toward me and stops so close that I can smell her. Focus, David.

"One, this is the last time tonight I am holding the door for you. That only happens when we're being social, which we are not right now. We have a job. Well, I have a job. With what comes next, you do not want my eyes or hands doing anything but what they are trained to do.

"Two, I cannot and will not wait for you. Your sister's and my mother's lives may depend on what I am about to do, so there is no waiting. Okay with you?"

She nods agreement, or possibly is impressed with my counting skills.

"Three, don't ever touch the bag unless I tell you to."

The bag is always black, with lots of pockets, and comes with the job and is never far from me. Unfortunately, every skateboarder or hipster wannabe these days carries something similar-looking, so it is not always as easy as it used to be to recognize operators by the bag they carry.

The bag is to carry things you need to get a particular job done, without overloading yourself: small binoculars; a small first-aid bag; extra ammo; extra batteries; cameras, one throwaway, one digital; sometimes a laptop or tablet computer; untraceable cell phone; a throwaway gun; Gore-Tex pullover;

extra cash; and duct tape for the real emergencies. You never know when Homeland Security is going to require that I tape myself in the bathroom or something equally exciting.

I'm still holding the door open. She just stands there. I raise my eyebrows.

"I shouldn't get in the car without knowing your name. My mother would kill me."

"My name is David Gibson," I say with a heavy sigh.

Finally, she climbs in the car. I cannot tell if she was serious.

I power up the 6.2-liter, header-backed-mufflered, enhanced-motored piece of craftsmanship and head to airport Command Center and Major Fuller.

We pull up in front of the building that houses the Command Center. There's no guard posted out front as is procedure. It's all happening way too fast and the guy who is supposed to be standing here is probably stuck in famous Boston traffic, or maybe the duty roster is not posted, or the cell phones don't work, or he is taking a piss. It doesn't matter. This is a serious place, I'm doing God's work tonight and I need to get ready to hear confession.

His name was David Gibson. At least, if he turned out to be a serial killer, I'd know what to scrawl on the wall in my own blood.

The car stopping, his pocketing of the key and his moving halfway across the lot to the front of the building was a series of efficient and effortless movements that seemed rehearsed. I was still wrestling with the seat belt he'd made me wear.

I pushed against the door and it didn't move. Checked to see if the door was locked; it wasn't. Must be stuck. After I leaned against it with my shoulder and pushed with all my weight, it finally opened. It was twice as hard to get it closed. He really needed to get this thing fixed.

I ran to catch up and followed him down the hall, past what seemed to be perfectly functioning elevators, then through a door marked STAIRS. He started up and his pace never slowed.

The only running I've ever done is run a campaign. My idea of exercise is lifting a giant cup of coffee to my lips and holding myself upright against gravity. I'm blessed with a great metabolism, but skinny doesn't necessarily equal fit.

Not wanting to fall behind, I kept up for an entire flight and a half. By the time we reached the fifth floor, I was sweating and close to hyperventilating. I was really beginning to dislike David Gibson.

"Any reason you're opposed to elevators?" I gasped.

"They're dangerous, for one thing, a potential trap. And if they stop, we stop. Could be two minutes or two hours. Either way, it's wasted time. From now on we steer clear of anything that can stop us or slow us down."

Hard to argue with that.

"Plus the stairs are better exercise, something I gather you know very little about."

When he turned around I stuck my tongue out at him. Not very mature, but I've always thought maturity was highly overrated.

He opened the door and we walked down the hall. The room at the end was buzzing with voices. I stepped closer to him.

"Where exactly are we?"

My voice was the hushed one I use in church and libraries. This place had that same feel of tension and authority.

"Command Center."

Well, that cleared everything up. Command Center for what? Was it always here or did it just magically pop up when there was an emergency?

There was a slightly different vibe coming off him now. Somewhere between the top of the stairs and the door to the Command Center something in David Gibson had shifted, and I sensed that now would not be a good time to ask for a tour and a history lesson.

"A friend of mine, name of Mark Fuller, is here. I have known him for six years; he is tough, straight, no-bullshit and not political. He runs this place and he owes me his ass."

From the hallway I could see inside the room. Uniformed people buzzed about trading pieces of paper and speaking in low, measured tones lost amid the shrill buzz of radios squawking, phones ringing and computers chirping. The room had the intensity of a campaign headquarters on election night, but with less chaos and shorter haircuts. I may have been out of my element but was determined not to look overwhelmed. An armed guard the size of a pickup blocked the door.

"I need to talk to Major Fuller."

"He's busy right now."

"Just tell him Colonel Gibson is here." The guard walked inside of the room, presumably to find Major Fuller.

"Why are we here?"

"To find out what they know."

"Oh. You're a colonel."

"I am."

"The kind who wears stars on his shoulders or the kind who knows which eleven herbs and spices?"

"The insignia for a colonel of the U.S. Army is a silver eagle. No stars."

I may know a bunch of these guys because I trained them, but I am retired and I have zero authority here. My immediate greeting and follow-up will be critical to us getting cooperation. When Major Fuller approaches, I go with some relaxed humor.

"So, Fuller Brush Man, how they hanging?" This is a good man, state police for seventeen years, his father a Boston cop, brother a detective in Brockton, your basic good man and a friend.

"Colonel, what brings you to my party?"

"Mark, my mother is on that plane."

"Shit. Sorry, sir. What do you need?"

Fuller escorts us past the guard and into the room. It is typical government style: chairs, computers, walls, desks, all gray. Even the hair on the men in the pictures that line the walls is gray.

We are not supposed to be in here, but I trained these guys, so everyone is dutifully ignoring that fact.

"What's the status on the flight?"

"At fifteen forty-five the hijackers radioed us. They said that they had taken control of the plane and that they would contact us in an hour. The pilot activated the microphone in the cockpit at fifteen forty-nine. Since then we've heard a few phrases, sounds like Arabic, but other than that they're not talking. No one here speaks Arabic. Our guy is on his way, but it could take him a while."

"So it's for real. This is a straight-up hijacking. They're not trying to take off. They're not talking, meaning they probably know about the microphone, meaning they're not stupid. How long until you get this place set up?"

"It's supposed to be up in two hours. We're fifteen minutes past that and probably another hour away."

"Shit! Anything I can do?"

"This is FBI jurisdiction. Mulligan is the ASAC. We're minutes away from him taking over and assuming responsibility for the Command Center and the incident. When that happens, you know you're out of here," he says in a low voice.

Okay, so the FBI is going by the book. No surprise there. The assistant special agent in charge (ASAC), the number two guy in New England for the FBI stationed here in Boston, is normally the guy who would show up at the Command Center this early.

This plane thing will be a federal matter quick. When this is declared a terrorist incident, and I bet it already has been, the authority to make this go away rests with the FBI. Mulligan is capable enough, but my bet is that he, like Fuller, will be getting more help here than he could have ever imagined. So far, this place is working pretty much as it should.

"Have you started your shifts yet?"

During a crisis, everyone wants to be involved all the time. People forget that human beings don't function well without sleep. One of the first things you do in a crisis is send some guys to bed, so when the first group can't think straight anymore, someone is fresh and ready to take control.

"Yup. Relax, Colonel. We'll do everything we can to get your mother off the plane safely.

"We're following the Emergency Assault Plan. We're doing everything you trained us to do. Snipers and observers are being positioned. Hospitals and EMS have been notified. SWAT is in the airport staging area prepping.

"Colonel, you helped us design this place. All those weekends, you ran all those hijacking training exercises for us right here. We owe you, and I remember that. Come with me. We'll get the latest."

He looks back at Christina.

"You too, Legs."

9

I know he didn't just call me Legs. David I-was-a-Colonel Gibson gave a look at Fuller that said, *Knock it off.* Not sure yet how I feel about that.

Fuller was about five-eight and wore a crew cut. He had fair skin, dark hair and the typical state police build. He thought he was pretty hot stuff. I resisted the temptation to ask him when the state police did away with the height requirement.

The room really did look like something off a movie set. I guess movie people hired technical advisors for a good reason. There were three rows of desks, all facing a wall with more television screens and monitors than an electronics store.

These guys all spoke their own language. Words without vowels or with vowels in funny places constituted whole phrases here. Things like *ASAC* obviously meant stuff to these guys. I was seriously at a disadvantage and no one thought to act as a military/police-to-human translator.

Major Fuller told us that everything at Logan was grounded and that they were bringing planes in all over the country. Since 9/11 they didn't fool around.

I listened and for the first time the reality of all this hit me: hijackers, Arabic, hospitals and EMS, snipers, SWAT. Holy shit! I pinched myself hoping I'd wake up, but all I got was a red mark that promised a nasty bruise.

I hoped my sister was being smart. Colleen is not a study in calm, cool and collected. She is quick to fly off the handle and kind of enjoys her anger. Sometimes I'm actually jealous of her ability to tell the world to fuck off and not care about the consequences.

I didn't think that was a good plan for today.

Fuller and David were still standing around talking.

There had been a lot of talking and absolutely no action. I stifled the urge to scream, *How about somebody do something?* I really was wondering how long we were going to stand around telling each other what we didn't know. Cable news did that. I was kind of hoping for a little better performance from the police.

In the movies, very handsome men in tight black pants carrying really big guns save the day. Where were they? Were they on a break? Where were the guys who storm the plane, kill the bad guys and rescue my sister?

GIBSON

We walk through the room, stopping at each desk asking for an update. Each of the desks is staffed with a liaison officer from a different government agency. Each one adding dots to the picture but with no one connecting them.

There are the Federal Aviation Administration liaison, airline liaison, Boston Police liaison, medical support liaison, Massport liaison, mayor of Boston representative, Mass National Guard representative, state police officers from SWAT, FBI representatives, and press liaison, just to name a few. There will be over sixty federal and state agencies trying to help resolve this. Sometimes it will be organized chaos, other times it will be just plain chaos.

State police have three hundred officers coming in to help. Massport is focused on the plane but also can't make radio contact with a liquid nitrogen gas (LNG) tanker carrying thirty thousand gallons of highly volatile gas outside of Boston Harbor. It has been out of contact for twenty minutes, not necessarily unusual. The guy is probably asleep. Boston PD reports rush-hour traffic on top of holiday traffic, which equals gridlock. The city is at a crawl.

The CIA and NSA will be here somewhere, trying to take credit for everything that goes well while blaming the locals for everything that does not.

"Hey, Brush Man, where are the intel guys, the spooks, the shadow watchers?"

Fuller rolls his eyes and motions us out of the room. We follow him through a door next to a mirror that is obviously two-way. The room is the same as the other one except it is smaller, quieter and smells bad; maybe that's just because these are intel people, it's hard to say. The room is full of computers and STU-III phones so that the staff can talk to other intelligence people in a secure mode.

The CIA can be the best intelligence agency in the world, bar none. Ever since 1980, when they were pulled in kicking and screaming to support Olympic events, the CIA has become part of the furniture in a crisis. They are dedicated government workers who deal in real-time, gut-wrenching information that the President of the United States gets daily. When they are good, they are very, very good and we never hear about it, and when they are bad, it's front-page news.

The guy in the corner doesn't look up when we come in and his computer has the little black box on it like the ones I've seen at Langley. It's called Tempest and basically it allows the computer to encrypt all messages, all work product going out and coming into it.

"Are all these guys connected? Are all the agencies talking?"

I already know the answer will be no.

"Listen, Colonel, it hasn't gotten any better. I know that the message has been that we are all working together. Ah, hell, watch this."

Major Fuller walks over to the CIA representative and asks, "So, Jerry, what do you have?"

Jerry, if that is his real name, first closes the cover on his computer and then turns to Fuller and says, "Nothing to report."

I can't help myself.

"So, Jerry, you mean no analysis of the voices on the plane? No passenger list comparisons? No offer of technical assistance or to contact the NSA and DIA for us to see how they can help? No speeches about how you are the DCI's representative and don't really have to talk to us . . . Jerry, where are you going?"

Jerry has left the room.

"I see you haven't lost your gentle touch, Colonel," says Fuller.

"Damn, Mark, nothing changes. We can't do this without the assholes and they know it. I promise you this: the deal will not go down well unless we get *Jerry* energized or replaced. Between him and the FBI, this is about to turn into an organized cluster and all the good information and good air is going to be sucked right out of room."

Major Fuller excused himself from the room for a minute. Phone call, pizza delivery, nuclear attack, who knows? I took a deep breath and exhaled.

Usually I would have been screaming and waving my hands, pushed to the point of hysteria by stress and caffeine withdrawal. But since the place was full of guys with guns who actually hadn't impressed me as all that bright, I wasn't yelling. Instead, I was doing that talk-through-your-teeth thing my mother always did when we misbehaved in public. She'd clench her teeth, and in a low, scary voice tell us to knock it off or we'd be sorry.

"Listen, I've been very good. I've been quiet and followed all the rules. All the dials in your car—and your bag—remain untouched. Major Fuller called me Legs and he's still walking around with all his parts, which I'll have you know required great restraint on my part. What I'd really like now is for you to explain to me *in English* what all of this means.

"From what I can tell, no one has told you anything you didn't know, except that the traffic in Boston at four o'clock on the Friday after Christmas really sucks, which I could have told you without the aid of four billion dollars' worth of computers. Oh, and there is a container ship full of liquid natural gas somewhere near us out of radio contact. How all of this helps, I really couldn't begin to fathom. My sister is on a plane. She's not on a boat. She's not in a car. She's on a plane."

Great! Now I was beginning to sound like Dr. Seuss.

"It's been almost three hours. At some point, and that point is rapidly approaching, I'm going to have to call my family and tell them that I put my sister on a plane that has been hijacked. I know you can't possibly understand this, but somehow they are going to think this is my fault. Which is absolutely ridiculous, I know. I mean, we're not close, and no, I didn't want to drive her to the airport, but I didn't want her to get hijacked either . . . Anyway . . . the point is, I'd really like to be able to tell them that something is being done to save her. I really don't want to have to tell them that I've run off with some colonel who seems to think its great fun to piss off the CIA guy."

I took a deep breath.

"And I really need a cup of coffee."

The look on his face told me I had slipped over the edge into total lunacy. He put his hand on my elbow and steered me into the hallway. And I let him.

I'm not sure if it's genetics or conditioning, but the women in my family are kind of an independent, feisty lot. We were raised to be competent and in charge and take no crap from anyone. Batting your eyelashes and acting helpless is strictly prohibited and I only break that rule when I have car trouble. Apparently I was confusing Colonel Gibson with a mechanic.

Everything about this guy should have been driving me crazy. He was giving me orders, physically moving me around and I could tell he was about to do the stern lecture routine again. I should have been really pissed off, but I wasn't. Some weird girly gene was rearing its ugly head.

He spoke quietly.

"First, in a contest of who wants their family off that plane the most, I win. Second, this is what I do. I have been fighting terrorists or training those that fight terrorists for the last twenty years. Again . . . this is what I do.

"You're right: coming here didn't tell us much that I didn't already suspect. Governments act a certain way when things go bad, so yeah, I could tell back at the airport that this was falling into the not-good box.

"Guys on the plane speaking Arabic and broken English telling you that they have your plane usually means a hijacking. That means that all this, everyone you are seeing and a ton of people you are not seeing should act in a prescribed manner. So now, instead of suspecting what's going on, I know.

"Fuller is going to come back and tell us the FBI has assumed control of the Command Center, so we're done. We're not going to get anything accomplished here. We need to start moving around. Are you still coming?"

I nodded. David Gibson had an answer for everything. He leaned in closer to me and I could feel his breath on my ear. The shaking thing stopped, and I was completely overwhelmed by how little distance separated us.

The thinking part of my brain decided to pick this moment to shut down. This guy was dangerous. What he did was dangerous. This was definitely bad news for me, because I didn't do dangerous. My body, however, was having thoughts of its own. My body was thinking dangerous might just be exciting.

"Yes, I'm coming with you."

"I will not let my mother or your sister die, if I have to take that plane myself."

12

Big green eyes look up at me. I thought she'd look afraid, but instead her eyes hold a challenge or maybe a promise, or maybe both.

For Christ's sake! My mother is being held hostage by terrorists and I'm having more than impure thoughts about a woman I've just met.

Fuller strides back down the hallway. He is pissed. These guys hate to be left out. The Bureau is a pain in the ass, but when it comes to assaulting a plane they are eons beyond the state police in any state.

"The Bureau is now in charge. I managed to get you a car and driver. Ms. Marchetti, here is my card if you need to reach me. It is only to be used in extreme duress. Now go meet my guy next to the C Terminal garage. He'll take you over to see the SWAT guys."

"Thanks, Mark. I'll call you from there."

I start to guide Christina down the hallway back toward the stairwell. She seems to have recovered from her moment, because she yanks her arm out of my hand. Fuller calls after me.

"Not for nothing, Colonel, but that tanker is still not responding. That's forty-five minutes with no contact and she's one hundred and twelve miles out. Not sure what it means."

Me, neither. I really want these guys to be thinking that anything can and probably will happen. A liquid natural gas tanker fully loaded traveling at fifteen knots slamming into, say, the Tobin Bridge would be a showstopper.

"Mark, I know you guys are watching all this crap. Just let me know how I can help."

I can tell the woman has something to say, but she waits until we exit the building.

"The tanker he was talking about? That's the boat?"

"It's more than a boat; if it blows up it will be a very bad day for Boston."

"How big a deal is it that it hasn't made contact in forty-five minutes?"

"It's a big deal."

She rolls her eyes and says, "Yes, thank you. A big deal."

She pauses for a breath while her eyes bore into me. "You may know a lot more than I do about what is happening here at the airport, but about that boat, Colonel, I know things as well. My boss, the senator, has been working to keep them out of Boston Harbor."

Her tone softens. "What do I need to know about that tanker?"

"Normally these tankers come and go in a harbor like Boston without most of us noticing. Pretty impressive, since these babies are four football fields long and up to eight stories high."

"Football fields and stories? You sure you weren't in the Navy?"

I didn't miss the sarcasm.

"You get the picture. So, the Coast Guard usually owns the water outside the harbor, while Massport along with the state and city police usually take the area from the breakwater to the dock."

"Again, I know all that. Why this tanker at this time?"

"Well, when the crap hits the fan, clear lines of responsibility sometimes get blurred, balls get dropped."

I see it sink in.

"So, the Coast Guard or the police are going to check it out and if something's wrong they'll fix it, right?"

She is trying to reassure herself. I am not in a reassuring mood.

"With a hijacking we have lots of experience. We have a fair idea of who is in charge and what to do from the good guy side. The heart of the problem is that outside of the SEAL community few really know how to handle a terrorist incident on the high seas. The Coast Guard and police are very good at boat theft, drug smuggling, refugees and the like, but terrorists taking a BFB? Nope, that would be your friendly neighborhood SEAL team."

"BFB?"

"Big fucking boat. I don't know if this tanker not talking to anyone is a terrorist thing, but if it is, this just got way more complicated."

She throws me a look that tells me I have not said what she wants to hear.

"You asked."

SECTION III

Everything in life is somewhere else,
and you get there in a car.

—E. B. WHITE

MARCHETTI

This day sucked already and now there was some runaway liquid natural gas tanker heading toward Boston. Okay, so I didn't know for sure it was a runaway, but Gibson seemed concerned and I was rapidly learning to trust his instincts. My instincts were screaming, *Run*, but that really didn't seem like a plan, since there wasn't anywhere to go.

We finally reached Terminal C and located the car that was waiting for us. The cold seemed to have gotten worse. I had morphed into a giant Popsicle. The only good thing about it was that my feet had gone numb and I couldn't feel just how badly they hurt. I climbed in the back of the car and David climbed in next to me. The front seat of the state police cruiser was filled with enough stuff to overload a small truck—computers, shotguns, notepads . . . and the biggest flashlight I had ever seen. I briefly wondered if this was referred to as a BFF—big fucking flashlight.

"Colonel Gibson, I'm Trooper Mullins. Major Fuller told me to take you where you want to go."

There was some brief exchange between them and the car started moving. I reached into my bag and pulled out my sneakers and a pair of socks. Nice, warm, thick, fluffy socks. If I were the type to have a spontaneous orgasm, the socks would have had me clinging to the roof of the car.

My bag is at least the size of a piece of carry-on luggage. Inside holds all the essentials and about ten years' worth of crap. I can rarely find the things I need and have on more than one occasion mistakenly tried to sign a check with a tampon that has come out of its wrapper. High heels have always seemed like a torture device to me, so unless I'm in a gown—which other than my cousin's wedding hasn't happened since my senior prom—I always carry my sneakers in my bag.

I unzipped my boots and tried to pull them off. The feeling in my feet started to come back, which on the good-bad spectrum was really, really bad. I had that frostbite-burning-pain-want-to-scream thing going on, and to top it off my feet had swollen up. I didn't think anything short of cutting the boots was going to get them loose.

I was yanking on the boots and unsuccessfully trying not to whimper when David looked over at me.

"What the hell are you doing?"

I wanted to hurt him. I was tired of feeling stupid. I was cold, scared, somewhere between done-in and exhausted, and wondering why I hadn't bothered to change into sneakers about an hour ago.

"I'm trying to get my boots off."

I had tried for that what-does-it-look-like-you-idiot? tone, but it came out sounding pathetic.

I covered my face with both hands and shook my head. This whole thing was ridiculous.

Why would anyone want to hijack this plane? Did it really need to be my sister's plane? Why? None of this made any sense.

I felt his hand on my calf and looked over at him. He gave a sharp tug on the boot and it was off. He pulled off the other one, and both feet were free.

I put the socks on and rubbed my feet. "Thank you."

"You're welcome."

GIBSON

I am beginning to sense real trouble with the tanker thing. It would be brilliant if these jerks did two things at once; a coordinated attack. A tanker has always been a real possibility and one we are largely unprepared for.

I'd better at least call Fuller and give it a try. I dial his cell phone.

"Mark, Dave Gibson. Look, I know you know this stuff, but if this tanker thing turns out to be butt-ugly, the closest SEAL team is four hours away in Virginia."

"Colonel, with all due respect, what drug are you on? You know it doesn't work that way. I will ask, but you and I both know what the answer will be: *Not my idea, therefore not a good idea,* or *We have already planned for that contingency.*"

"Yeah, I figured. Sorry to bother you, Mark."

I disconnect and want to eat the phone.

MARCHETTI

I tried to play it cool while Trooper Mullins did his best impression of Scotty pushing the starship *Enterprise* into warp speed, but truth is I am a lousy passenger.

When I was a little kid I would yell, "Mom, look out!" from the backseat, and she would almost kill us trying to react to whatever I thought was going to hit us, usually a tree or a house.

Now, control freak that I am, I almost always do the driving. When I'm forced to be a passenger, I clutch the "Jesus Christ" handle, which is the little doohickey that hangs down from the ceiling. It's probably really for hanging dry cleaning, but it doubles nicely as something to hold on to while praying or cursing. Praying isn't my strong suit, so usually I curse.

Unfortunately, cursing wasn't an option this time, and neither was hanging on to the little handle. I was so scared I couldn't remember any curse words and the car was doohickeyless.

4

When you get a good driver with a car that is weighted properly, with the right shocks, suspension, engine and transmission, it is a thing of beauty. Trooper Mullins is clearly trying to demonstrate that he and his ride are all that and more. I am impressed.

Unfortunately, Christina does not appreciate the finer points of pursuit driving. She is gripping my arm like a vise, and her fingernails are digging into my biceps. She is bracing herself with the other hand against the back of the driver's seat and she has gotten paler, which I didn't think was possible.

"Corporal, later on when it is just you and me in the car, you can drive fast enough so that it scares me, but right now let's appreciate that we have Ms. Marchetti back here. So unless you are chasing something on this empty airport access road, how about letting up a notch on the pedal?"

Trooper Mullins slows, more because we've arrived at the hangar than for any other reason.

To the untrained eye this place looks chaotic: black bags, Velcro, chewing tobacco, gun oil, subdued discussions, nervous tension—all expected and all totally professional. These are the boys in black who really do save the day.

The Massachusetts State Police Special Tactical Operations (STOP) Team is probably somewhere between standing up to deploy and sitting back down, because the FBI is now in charge. Truth is, these boys know the deal and will roll with all the punches.

The SWAT thing started in California. The Los Angeles police asked the Marines to help them with tactics and different weapons. To this day L.A. has one of the best SWAT teams in the country and it's full-time. SWAT is all they do.

These guys in the hangar are full-time state police, riding in cars or riding a desk. They are, at least, double volunteers. They first volunteer to be state police, then they put their hands up and volunteer to be on this Special Tactical Operations Team. They train weekly and sometimes the training is worse than the real thing. They do this very dangerous job without complaint or hardly a second thought. They used to be part-time, but for the past few years and because of 9/11 they are now a full-time unit, which means they are pretty damn good.

He swore under his breath.

"What's wrong?" I asked in a low tone.

"Look! Some of them are wearing wedding rings. Some are wearing watches. These are basic no-nos. They get caught on things and then you lose a knuckle or wrist and the team is then short a man or two."

Lose a knuckle? I really could have done without the visual.

"Goddamn it! There is even a shotgun out there. A shotgun in a plane." David was beside himself.

I knew I didn't really want to know why the shotgun was a bad thing, but I asked anyway.

"The shotgun? Not a good idea?"

"Look, Ms. Marchetti, a shotgun is mainly a spray-'em weapon, unless you use a slug. That's a big bullet, to you. Even then, it's not the most accurate thing in the world. It is a long gun. It catches on things. It is indiscriminate, not surgical like a MP5 or M4. With a shotgun you shoot the bad guy and my mother at the same time. *Capiche?*

"When you are moving men and guns inside a cone or cylinder, which is essentially what a plane is shaped like, you want yourself as streamlined as possible: nothing but things that are sleek; things that don't weigh a lot; things that shoot straight; and things that don't catch on other things, like slings, rings and big watches."

David walked out of earshot and talked to one of the guys. When he returned, he was more pissed off than he had been about the whole lose-a-knuckle thing.

"The assholes on that plane have a guy coming out the back stairs and walking around. That makes any approach up the ass end of the plane problematic. That guy has to go."

Uh-huh. Sure.

He strode off back toward the door, and once again I was hurrying after Colonel Gibson.

It was dark as we crossed the parking lot to the car. I had to jog to keep up with him and strain to hear him over the wind.

"These guys are totally focused on the hijacking and for my mother's sake that's good, but this situation does not feel right. This tanker? This large floating time bomb is not getting any attention. What we really need now are the SEALS, but we're not going to get them until it's too late."

I grunted because I was out of breath and incapable of speaking. We reached the car, he climbed in and I collapsed into the backseat.

"Mullins, I need to get to my car.

"Your boys look great!" I reassured him, "They are very capable and it's good they're here if the HRT is late." I could be wrong, but it now looked as if he was simply lying.

Gibson turned and looked at me. "The team that will eventually arrive and take over this situation will be the Hostage Rescue Team of the FBI. Their team is trained by Delta Force and SEAL Team Six, the very same guys who killed bin Laden. Those two units are the best special operations forces in the world, period."

I nodded because I couldn't think of an appropriate response; and because I didn't want him to know I still hadn't caught my breath. I wasn't exactly sure when Gibson had started explaining things without me having to pull it out of him, but I was grateful. I was beginning to think that he might be human after all.

I fumbled through my purse, dragged out my phone and hit the 1 on speed dial.

6

As we drive within sight of the plane, Christina has chosen this moment to chat on the phone. Can't imagine to whom, but I really don't care. Mullins tells me that there have been no changes in the last fifteen minutes.

The phone disappears back into the purse and she grabs my arm.

"What's that?"

"Where?"

"Moving in the window . . . there!"

She points to a window toward the back of the plane. The shade is going up and down.

"Mullins! Stop here."

I reach into my bag and pull out a pair of high-powered miniature binoculars. Focusing on the window, I can see a sign. It reads t6.

Her eyes plead with me to tell her what is happening and why, and to tell her everything will be okay. I might be able to tell her what and why, but the okay part would be guessing. She is scared.

"Nice job, Christina. Trooper, how about you calling Major Fuller and telling him that there are six terrorists on board, at least?"

"How do we know that?" the corporal asks.

All the training that has been done since 9/11 with airline employees may just be paying off. One of the classes being taught is how to signal information outside the plane. Putting a note on the outside of a window shade is simple but effective. Coming up with the code was easy—t for *terrorist* and a number telling how many—getting that code disseminated throughout the airline industry and the counterterrorist community was trickier. Hell, getting these super-sized, self-important government agencies to exchange phone numbers is a goddamn miracle.

"The sign in the window."

Mullins radios Fuller and tells him about the sign.

"Major Fuller said thanks and that the sniper observers spotted the number about the same time, but to tell you and the babe, nice, very nice."

He then drops us off at my Cadillac. I hit the button to disengage the locks. Christina struggles against the weight of the door, finally opens it and climbs in. She is talking into her cell phone, trying to calm down someone named Mary Katherine.

"It's okay. It's going to be fine. Has the senator gotten back to you yet?"

I call Fuller.

"Brother Fuller, I'd like to tell you this is the last favor, but that would be bullshit. I need you to get me and Ms. Marchetti out of your airport; can you get us cleared?"

He does and we're on our way.

Let's see, my saintly mother is being threatened on a plane and I can't do anything about it. There is a huge liquid natural gas tanker that is somewhere near Boston Harbor that no one can talk to. I have a woman attached to me but for all the wrong reasons and I can't shoot anyone yet. Oh, yeah, did I mention I want to kill something? I have a wicked sense that we are in for a very bad night.

MARCHETTI

Once this was all over, I decided I was getting a physical. I wasn't used to running, so the out-of-breath thing I understood. What I didn't understand was why I was having such trouble opening the car door. I was thirty-two years old; opening a car door should, at this stage in my life, have been effortless. Instead, I pulled every muscle in my right arm. I hoped there was no permanent damage.

Gibson was doing the strong, silent thing again but with even more intensity, and this time I was glad. My brain was on overload. Flashing red lights and a robotic voice saying, "Danger, Will Robinson! Danger!" floated through my head. I took a minute to try to remember the name of the TV show that it was from, but it wouldn't come.

My left arm was braced against the dash, since lifting the right one was out of the question. We were hauling ass. Gibson was weaving in and out of traffic and moving around anything in our way. His face and demeanor were set at steely determination. Mine were somewhere between overwhelming terror and resigned acceptance that we were going to die.

"If you survive the fiery crash we're headed for and I don't, tell my mom I want yellow roses at my funeral. None of the Italian red carnation crap." The words came out through clenched teeth.

"Not now, rookie. In case you have not noticed, we are going rather fast. There are terrorists in control of a plane with our family members on it, and you want to talk about, what? Flowers? If you have someplace else to be, please let me know where and I will drop you off."

He paused and then in a cocky voice said, "Oh, and I do know what the hell I am doing, so trust me."

Ha! I had heard that before.

"I used to know a guy who was in the Coast Guard who would get women to go to bed with him by saying, 'Trust me, the government does.' So forgive me if I'm a little underwhelmed by men who think they know what they are doing."

"Did that kind of line really work with you? You seem smarter than that."

It was my turn to be silent.

8

GIBSON

She is quiet for all of thirty seconds, and then the questions start.

"Why do you think they are doing this? Why Boston? Why this plane? I don't get it. What do you think they want?"

I am finished answering questions.

"Look, you are very smart. You are good-looking enough to cause trouble, and you have a personal reason for being here. I respect that. But I am spending more time telling you things than helping this situation."

She rolls her eyes at me.

"Marjorie P. Gibson is on that plane and I will kill a lot of people and dump your pretty ass in the ocean before I lose her to a bunch of terrorist assholes."

She's not listening. She's dialing her phone again.

"Mary Katherine, any word?"

I figure the phone call will keep her busy and distract her from playing twenty questions, but I am wrong.

"Where are we going and why?"

That's it. No more. I pull the car hard to the right. The tires make a screeching sound. I turn in my seat, meet her eyes and give her my best scary-colonel glare. I wait for the shaking and tears. It doesn't work. She is holding her cell phone to her ear.

I grab the steering wheel and squeeze so hard the leather makes a popping sound.

She looks at me like I'm having a seizure and she can't tell why. I look down and don't say anything for about ten seconds.

"You and I are only here together because our families are in trouble. In any other scenario, our worlds would never touch. Ever. And that would be fine with me, but you asked me if you could come along and I was dumb enough to agree."

This woman is driving me crazy. Half the time I want to grab her spectacular ass, the other half I want to kick it. Right now I want her gone. The cell is still to her ear.

"Listen, call your mother, call one of your political boy-friends or lawyer lovers or whomever to come and get you—or walk home, for all I care—but you and I are done. You can read all about it in the paper in the morning. Get out."

"I'm on hold. I got through to Senator Kerrigan and ex-plained to him what's going on. He's on the other line with the chief of naval operations at the Pentagon."

She sits straight up, all the while holding my gaze.

The senator must have come back on the line because she starts nodding into the phone.

"Yeah, I'm here. Okay, wait a second . . ."

She covers the phone again.

"He says the Atlantic fleet commander out of Norfolk can order a surprise call-out training exercise in the Boston area for the SEAL assault platoon. You know, test their readiness. Listen, I don't speak military and we don't have time for me to learn a new language, I'm assuming you know what that means?"

"Chris, that is the best news we have had since your boots came off. I guess they don't want to call the tanker missing yet since we're not really sure but having a SEAL platoon with over thirty of the best operators in the world, available and in position to hit that tanker, just put a plus in the good guys' column. Make sure you keep that senator happy."

"Oh, so you would like for that to happen?" There is a mock-ing tone in her voice.

I know where this is going.

"Yes."

She turns back to the phone, says, "That sounds like a great idea. Thank you, sir," and disconnects. She throws the cell into her black hole of a bag.

Maybe keeping her and her connections around isn't the worst thing. Moving a SEAL team with a phone call is pretty impressive. Even I can't do that. I am not doing well with this woman. Time to stop thinking about this. Time to start killing things and saving the world.

I hit the gas.

For the first time since this whole thing started, I was feeling useful, like I could make a difference. Being useless or—worse—dead weight to be carried was a feeling I hated. I didn't want to be ornamental, a fashionable accessory, Colonel Gibson's giant purse. I contemplated explaining this to Gibson but realized his idea of an accessory came in different calibers. Focus, Christina. What should we do next? It sank in that we were, in fact, doing something.

"Wait. Why are we driving away from the airplane? The place where my sister, your mother and at least six angry terrorists are?"

"You think we'll help storm the plane? Is that your thought here?"

"Well, not, umm, no, probably not."

"We can't help there. But something doesn't add up here, so we're going to double-check the math."

"'Double-check the math,'" I say in the deepest, gravelliest voice I can manage. "You must be getting tired. Your manly quotes need work."

"Look, a tanker not responding should be causing a stir. A tanker carrying liquid natural gas stops responding, and the Coast Guard should be swinging into action with everything they have. I'm starting to think this whole thing may be about that. Your sister and my mother may be nothing more than a distraction."

"So, what are we doing?"

"I'm going to the North End Coast Guard Station. You're in the car."

GIBSON

The Cadillac whips down a narrow street into a parking lot with the Coast Guard station on the right and a baseball field under a few inches of gray snow on the left. The ocean is a shimmering of reflected light on inky blackness in front of us.

She's sitting there giggling to herself. "'Double-check the math.' Carry the one. Subtraction is addition's tricky pal."

I'd think she's losing it, but I'm not sure she ever had it. To be fair, she's in over her head and the adrenaline has to wear off sometime. She's holding up better than I expected and that trick with the SEAL team, if it actually happens, is worth all the trouble she gives me. Plus she hasn't yet touched the radio.

Putting the storage compartment in the Cadillac was worth the cost. Duke said it would come in handy and he was right. I've got long guns with ammo; an M4 with ACOG 4x optical sight with plenty of black-tipped, armor-piercing ammo; extra SIG P228 and 9mm hollow-point ammo. The hollow-point stuff is ideal for urban fighting, since it will go through a car engine if need be, to say nothing of body armor and the people wearing it. Less exciting but just as necessary are the commo gear, cameras, extra clothes, nightscopes, first-aid bag, and duct tape—can't do the terrorist thing without duct tape.

When I'm done with my mental inventory I notice she's quiet.

"You done now?"

"I am."

"Good, because we're here."

The Cadillac whips down a narrow street up by a long, high chain-link fence. The guard booth at the front gate was empty and this side entrance is also deserted. I pull the Escalade over by a broken street lamp. Fifty-nine hundred pounds of Detroit steel disappear into the puddled darkness of a side street in Boston's North End.

"Chris, stay put."

SECTION IV

You see something scary, you should stand up and step toward it, not away from it. Instinctively, reflexively, in a raging fury.

—LEE CHILD, *Echo Burning*

He walked around to the back of the car, opened the rear door and started rummaging around. There was no way I was staying put. If I stayed put, I might miss something. I hate it when I miss something. I angled the door open and winced as I pushed on it, hard.

Gibson was sorting through a hidden compartment in the back of his car. It was full of guns, knives, ropes and a bunch of other things I couldn't even begin to identify.

I did a small mathematical equation. Guns + fear = wise-ass comment.

"Does this all come standard with the Cadillac or do you have to pay more?"

"So much for staying put," he snarled, but he didn't look up. He was putting on some kind of holster with Velcro straps and a black vest. I was about to make a snarky comment about the vest when he put a gun in the holster. I knew nothing about guns, except that they killed people. I was usually politically and personally opposed to guns and killing, so I stifled the joke. He grabbed a roll of black tape and started taping down his pants. My mouth engaged before my brain could stop it.

"What's the tape for?"

"Anything loose can catch on things and make noise."

"The lose-a-knuckle principle with a twist. Gotcha!"

Sometimes my mouth annoyed even me.

"I am going in there to see what is going on. You need to be here ready to call the police if necessary. Stay in the car and lock the doors. The car is bulletproof; you will be safe. I'll be back out in sixteen minutes. If I am not out, drive away and call the police."

He grabbed a really big, scary-looking gun. It was almost three feet long and screamed, *Kill 'em all*. I was pretty sure Senator Kerrigan had voted against a bill that gave your everyday average citizen the right to own one of these. But then again, Colonel David Gibson was hardly your average anything. Right before my eyes he had transformed into Danger Dave the action figure, complete with Kung Fu Grip.

I climbed back into the car, locked the doors and looked at the clock on the dashboard. 8:07 P.M. I squinted into the dark trying to see him, but I couldn't. He was gone. Random thoughts skittered around my head, not the least of which was: Where do you buy a bulletproof car?

2

GIBSON

It's a funny part of Boston. A modern major road holds back old neighborhoods of typical Boston three-story houses turned into rentals, a few seedier apartment buildings and some old brown brick buildings of such a nondescript nature you have to focus just to even notice them. On the other side of the road are docks and beautiful harbor walks and fancy tourist restaurants, along with a working base for the United States Coast Guard, the headquarters for the First District of the USCG, as a matter of fact.

I take my M4 carbine: compact, lightweight, and projects a variable-intensity red dot to pretty much infinity. You have to remember to keep both eyes open when using this system, unlike a regular sight in which you use only your good shooting eye. The thing that differentiates guys like me, who do what I do, is our willingness to go through the door without hesitation with both eyes open.

I take a SIG P228 too. It is a 9mm automatic handgun that out of the box is the most accurate and durable handgun made, although around gun guys the SIG 226 gets good grades as well. I just like the weight of the 228. I like this gun and the M4. They work all the time, every time. I grab the AN/PVS-5, a night-vision device; extra magazines for the M4; BOSS ballistic goggles; Blackhawk Hellstorm gloves; and check the SureFire tactical light mounted on the M4. I also bring a cell phone with an embedded encryption device, which allows me to bounce necessary phone calls off specific satellites. These friends have saved my ass more than once. All set. I start to move.

I take a quick walk around the place. It's a significant base, but when ships are deployed in the harbor, it may not be a really well-manned building. The ships are probably deployed now since the liquid natural gas tanker is out of communication. Between that and the holidays, I'm thinking it's a skeleton crew, but that still wouldn't explain seeing no one by the guard station. It's an easy six stories high, maybe more, so my first hope is to find the fire escape. Always better to go downhill if you think there may be shooting. Moving down on others with weapons in their hands gives me an advantage. Guys with less training usually don't have the shooting skills to be accurate when shooting up and at unusual angles or in low light. Coming down on a target also gives me some momentum. I certainly am not going in the front door. You never use the front of anything in this business, unless, of course, you have a tank. It is too obvious.

The fire escape should be locked and it's not. Someone else had already gone top-down. I'll have to find another way in. If you can't go top-down, you find the basement and try for the opposite of what they expect. Surely no one is stupid enough to come all the way up from the basement! Try me.

The building faces out toward the water over some parking lots and docks. The "rear" of the building is on the major road. I find an old small door on Commercial Street locked up tight. It's risky, but I shoot through the lock and slip in. I hold my breath, waiting to see if anyone heard and comes running. Nothing. I start moving down the darkened hallway. I am hugging the wall, staying out of the open, moving deliberately, heel-toe, heel-toe. The M4 is off safe, with a round chambered, ready. The gun butt is deep into my right shoulder and is pointed wherever my eyes go. I soon realize why no one heard my entrance. There's nothing here except that smell. It is one you never . . . ever forget.

It is death: burning body parts, guts out, bowels that have let go.

No bodies in any of the offices. All the phones are dead. The computers are not working. I need to check the basement power units. Twelve minutes left at best before Christina hits the panic button and calls the cops.

I make my way down the stairs. They are all in the basement: Coast Guard kids, officers and noncommissioned officers. It looks like there are a few civilians, maybe visitors, maybe family. Doesn't matter anymore. I count thirteen. They are all dead.

Some have been shot twice through the thoracic cavity. The chest is a large target. A shot there hits the lungs most of the time and the heart some of time. Many have been double-tapped just to make sure; very deadly and very professional. One is shot in the back, another in the head. Must have surprised a couple and got them running. There are some bruises; a couple must have put up a fight.

I really want to kill something.

MARCHETTI

It was rapidly approaching the sixteen-minute mark. I was all about precision, but sixteen seemed like a totally arbitrary number. And was I supposed to call the police at 8:23 or wait until the full minute had passed until 8:24? Should we have synchronized watches? This was stupid. Nothing had happened since he'd gone in there. No gun noises, no explosions, no mass fleeing of people out of the building. He was probably in there doing more of the macho-colonel routine, asking people how they're hanging.

I slammed my body against the door and it opened. I had been sitting in the driver's seat, so this time it was the left shoulder that took the bruise. I briefly weighed the pros and cons of having to open a bulletproof door vs. getting shot.

I walked up to the front door of the building and tried to squint through the glass. I couldn't see anything. The moon wasn't throwing much light and it was pitch-black inside. I opened the door and took a step.

Holding my breath, I didn't hear anything, not a drip from a faucet, not even a hum from a refrigerator. Nothing. I stuck my hand out in front of me and slowly felt my way down a corridor. I stopped, squinted and listened. There was still nothing to hear, but now there was the smell. I've read enough books and watched enough late-night television to recognize that a dark building + girl all alone + bad smell = a dead body.

Coming in here had been a mistake. My brain was saying, *Turn around and RUN!* when something about the air in the room changed.

The hair on the back of my neck stood up. Someone was there. I could feel it.

There is probably a list of things one should do in this situation. Run. Scream. Wet your pants. I froze. I absolutely could not move. I tried but nothing happened. My heart was pounding and I had stopped breathing. Somewhere out in the darkness, I half saw what looked like a tiny beam of light. I looked down at my chest and there was a little red dot.

GIBSON

Movement above me. I hit the stairs at the opposite end of the hallway from the noise. I back up the stairs, looking up. I crouch and then crawl to the top because coming out of a stairwell or a doorway is a nice way to get shot. I have this great view of sneakers and jeans, and then the legs and beyond. I stand up and point the M4 at her and turn the laser on her chest.

She does not see me. I move forward until I am so close the M4 is almost touching her. She is in the dark and I can see perfectly with my night-vision goggles. I move the M4 down and sling it over my back. She was supposed to stay in the car. I only asked for sixteen minutes.

I whisper, "Don't scream, it's me."

She screams anyway. I grab her and pull her down to the floor with my hand on her mouth.

She still does not know it is me. She tries to move me off her but only succeeds in aligning her body under mine. Not an entirely unpleasant experience, but really not the time.

I lean down and put my mouth on her ear.

At first I thought I'd fainted. It took a few seconds to realize someone had knocked me to the floor.

I tried to kick, punch, scratch, bite, anything to get free, but whoever was on top of me was way too strong. After all of that effort, the only thing I managed to do was wriggle underneath him a little.

"It's David and I need you to be calm."

His mouth was against my ear and I felt and heard him whisper, but it took a few seconds for the words to register. I was still trying to push him off me.

"I need you to stop."

I stopped moving, or tried to. I was shaking.

"Chris, there is a room full of dead people downstairs. We need to be gone from here now. We are probably safe. Whoever did this is not hanging around for door prizes. I'm going to take my hand away. When I do, get up but stay behind me. Keep your hand on my left hip all the way to the car. If I stop between here and the car, fall down or I will knock you down. Just nod your head if you understand."

I nodded and he took his hand away. He lifted himself off me and I stood. I put my hand on his hip and we moved down the corridor to the door and outside. We made it to the car and climbed in. I struggled with the door but barely noticed. Fear was winning.

My teeth were chattering even though I wasn't cold. I put my seat belt on and wrapped my arms around myself.

"Call the Boston PD and tell them what you saw. I'll call Fuller and fill him in." I turn left out of the Coast Guard station.

She fishes around in her purse and finds her phone.

"What exactly am I supposed to tell them? *Hi, this is Christina Marchetti, aide to Senator Kerrigan, and I just found a bunch of dead guys in the North End Coast Guard Station? Am I still there? Ah . . . no . . . sorry, I'm driving around Boston with Rambo.*"

"Don't tell them your name. It will complicate things. Just tell them what and where."

She makes a sound that is halfway between a groan and a sob, but she starts dialing. I pull out my phone and call Fuller.

"Mark. I am actually not sorry to be calling you because you are about to look real smart. I just left the Coast Guard station in the North End; the place is a killing field."

"Shit! How many?"

"At least thirteen dead, downstairs in the boiler room. There are no comms, no lights. The place is a graveyard. I am out of there, going to One Boston Place to check out a hunch. Before you ask me anything, are you getting any calls in from any first responders: Boston PD, EMS, fire? Anybody?"

"Nothing."

"Goddamn it! Didn't think so. What can you tell me about the plane?"

"No more movement. We have handed the situation over to the FBI, who are planning. In other words, frustration."

7

I admit it. I was freaked out. It's not every day I see a bunch of dead guys. Okay, so I didn't really see them, but I smelled them and I knew they were there. Then I'd been tackled by a dangerous man who turned out to be Gibson. I wasn't sure I hadn't wet my pants.

My back was sore from where I'd hit the floor under his weight, and I had a bump on my head. On top of it all, I was feeling really stupid for having gone into the building in the first place. I was also feeling a little inadequate, since I had discovered Colonel Gibson was strong enough to pin me with a mere glance. Freaked out was an understatement. I was bordering on hysteria.

It seemed nothing rattled this guy. I don't like being bested at anything. I pride myself on being able to handle a crisis. So I choked back tears, pretended to be calm and did what I was told.

I dialed 911 and hit send. Nothing happened. I tried again, and still nothing. I dialed a third time, and when it didn't go through, I fought back the urge to throw my phone. I checked the battery. It was charged. I looked over at Gibson, but he was focused on the road and his conversation with Fuller.

I decided to try another number to see if I could get through to anyone. Mary Katherine picked up on the first ring.

"It's Christina."

"Oh, my God! The senator told me your sister is on the plane that was hijacked. Are you all right?"

"I'm fine . . ."

"What's going on?"

"I need—"

"Everyone from home keeps calling, asking what's happening. I wouldn't tell them anything, of course . . ."

Mary Katherine wouldn't give away national secrets, intentionally; but she was one of the biggest gossips in Boston. This was quite a distinction, since in terms of Boston pastimes, gossip falls just below explaining why this is the year the Red Sox will win the Series and slightly above drinking green beer and brawling on St. Patrick's Day.

"Mary Katherine, you probably know more about what is going on at the airport because you have access to a TV. I don't know anything, but I need a favor."

"Shoot."

Interesting choice of words.

"I'm trying to dial 911. For some reason I can't get through. I need you to get in touch with the Boston police and tell them . . ."
Tell them what, exactly?

"Tell them what?" Mary Katherine echoed.

I took a deep breath.

"Tell them there has been a shooting at the North End Coast Guard Station and they need to get someone over there."

For the first time ever, Mary Katherine was speechless.

"Hello? Did I lose you?"

"Tell them what?"

I rolled my eyes.

"Tell them there has been a shooting over at the North End Coast Guard Station, but . . . don't tell them how you know. Don't mention my name."

"Oh, my God! You shot someone?"

There was awe in her voice.

I rolled my eyes again. This was getting ridiculous.

"No, I didn't shoot anyone. Please, just do it. I'll explain it all to you later."

"Okay. I'll call Michael and tell him. He's not going to be happy when I won't say how I know this. You're going to owe me big time."

"I know. I'm good for it."

I disconnected and blew out a sigh. Being beholden to Mary Katherine was a lifetime thing. I'd be paying for this forever. Maybe longer.

About one and a half miles from the Coast Guard station is the Emergency Management Center, where all of the emergency communications for the city of Boston are routed through. In other words, all of the emergency response units communications originate at, end, or pass through this building.

It is state-of-the-art and one of the dumbest moves ever conceived. If the building blows up, has a fire, dies of old age, or is attacked somehow, the city and all agencies, federal or otherwise, involved in any crisis would not be able to communicate by radio. They could still use cell phones, but in an emergency, those lines clog up fast.

Christina's head is turned away from me; she's looking out the window at six blue-and-whites headed down Congress Street. They are driving toward the Coast Guard station. She must have gotten through.

"There is something wrong with my cell phone. When I dialed 911, all I got was air. I called Mary Katherine and she called her brother Michael. He's a cop. He called them," she says in a flat tone.

That confirms my hunch. Someone has damaged the communications system.

She is still not looking at me. She needs to snap out of it. It's been hard so far, but my guess is, it's going to get worse. I need to get her attention and have her focus on the here and now.

"Look, Chris, I totally understand why you did not do as I

asked and stay in the car. Why would you? You clearly know more about this stuff than I do. Ahhh . . . no, you don't. I grant you that you are smarter, quicker with words, better connected, go to church more than I do, vote in every election and take in stray cats, but . . . if you don't do what I tell you to do, I will leave you where you stand and not think another thought of it or you."

She looks over at me and for a second; I think she is going to stick her tongue out at me. Instead, she just stares at me, then turns back to look out the window.

"Bite me," she says. There is some venom in her voice, so I guess she must be feeling a little better.

"'Bite me'? Did you just say, 'Bite me'? What are you, twelve?"

MARCHETTI

The "Bite me" comment had been reflex and stupid. Apparently that was my standard operating procedure for the day. He didn't even blink, just came back with a wiseass comment of his own. Usually I do okay when it comes to witty and wise-ass, but today I was in a battle of wits and I had come to it pretty much unarmed.

I was also feeling a tad immature, not because he said I sounded twelve, but because I actually hadn't started saying anything like "Bite me" until my early twenties. Who knew that at age thirty-two you could still feel like a late bloomer? I was definitely going to need therapy for all the ways I had discovered I was inadequate since I'd met David Gibson.

GIBSON

She turns and glares at me.

"Where are we going now?"

"We are going over near the mayor's office. It's a big building at One Boston Place. We need to know how far this thing has gone, or can go."

I step on the gas and her arm shoots out. She grabs my shoulder.

"Hold on to something besides me."

I turn left up State Street, bust through four lights at eighty miles an hour and turn left again in front of the Marriott and Tia's Restaurant. I'm looking for the first right I can take that will get me into downtown Boston, with its heart-attack-causing congested arteries and clots of pedestrians apparently unaware there are cars using the roads. Day-after-Christmas shoppers are not making this any easier. The one-way streets guaranteed to not be going the way you want are more than a little full with everyone trying to get a better deal than everyone else.

We pull in front of One Boston Place as if we own it. Officer You-Are-Not-Going-to-Park-Here comes over.

"What do you think you are doing? This is a no-parking zone, a one-way street and you are blocking everything."

I pulled out my not-supposed-to-have active duty military ID with the colonel thing written on it.

"Major Fuller from F Troop at Logan asked me to come over."

Officer No-Parking-Anywhere says, "Who the hell is Fuller and why do I care? Move the car, now."

MARCHETTI

Tommy McKenna was pushing forty and the cop diet he'd been on for the last twenty years was pushing at his uniform. He was six feet tall and about two hundred and fifteen pounds. Twenty pounds of it were made up of donuts and beer and had settled just north of his belt buckle. He was a friend of the senator's, a friend of mine and an all-around good guy. He was not intimidated or impressed by David Gibson.

Boston police, when they get their Irish up, don't care if you're the Pope or the President; if they say move the car, you move the car. Gibson did the ID-flashing thing and the name-dropping thing and then moved on to the steely stare and physically intimidating thing. It didn't help any. McKenna wasn't playing.

I undid the seat belt and stared at the door. It was laughing at me. I hated that door. I pulled on the handle, put both feet on the door and pushed as hard as I could with my legs. The door flew open and I jumped out. In my head were visions of Rocky Balboa reaching the top of the stairs and doing his victory dance. The music blared in my head and I smiled. Then the door swung back and caught my shoulder.

My vision blurred from tears and pain. I opened my mouth to scream but no sound came out. I gingerly put my left hand on my right arm and bent over at the waist, trying to wish the pain away. When the pain lessened enough for me to start breathing again, I righted myself.

"Hey, Tommy," I called weakly. Both Tommy and David turned. If either had witnessed the door incident, they didn't say anything. I was glad. Humiliating myself is something I excel at. That doesn't mean I am comfortable with it.

Tommy smiled and walked over to me, leaned over and kissed me on the cheek.

"How are you, Christina?"

"I'm fine. How are the girls?"

"Driving me crazy," he said, though his blue eyes twinkled, "but they're fine." Tommy McKenna had six kids age four through eighteen, all girls. He was crazy about them.

His expression changed to one of worry, and his voice lowered.

"You with this guy?"

"Yeah, he's okay."

Tommy looked doubtful and eyed David up and down again.

"You could do better."

"It's not like that, Tommy. Trust me. We need to go inside for a few minutes. I'd really appreciate it if you'd let us leave the car here."

"Sure. Not a problem."

"Thanks. We won't be long."

While Tommy and I were talking, David had walked to the back of the car and rummaged around. When he appeared beside me he was totally transformed. The big gun had been switched for a smaller one, I assumed, since I didn't see the scary thing, and he was now dressed in a long coat and a baseball cap. He was no longer Danger Dave; he was ordinary. Somehow he didn't look like the same person. No one you'd give a second glance. If only transformations were that simple for women. I usually needed forty-five minutes in the morning just to achieve a look that wouldn't frighten small children.

Tommy looked worried now.

"It's okay, Tommy. I promise," I said before he could ask about the master of disguise. "We'll only be a few minutes."

He nodded and assumed his cop face.

We walked into the building. The lobby was barely lit by emergency lights on backup power. The power was out, just like at the Coast Guard station. A shiver ran through me. David asked at the desk for the technical applications quality control officer. Apparently everyone in Colonel Gibson's world had a title that indicated his or her job description. It kind of reminded me of the movie

Dances with Wolves, where everyone had an Indian name. Kevin Costner was Dances with Wolves, the really cute Indian guy was Wind in His Hair. A guy I lived with briefly, after college, would have been Crumbs on Counter or Underwear on Floor. Anyway, the guy behind the counter should have been called No Help at All. He told us the power was out and to have a nice day.

GIBSON

"Hi, I am Colonel Gibson and I am not—repeat, *not*—having a nice day. I can tell you're not either, but I've been sent here to help."

It's not a total lie. I believe God has placed me here to figure out what is going on, find bad guys and shoot them repeatedly. So, yes, I have been sent to help. The kid looks at me with disbelief. I hold his stare and he suddenly seems grateful. Believing me is apparently easier than getting rid of me.

"Uh, Mr. Royce is in the office by the elevators looking at maps and using his cell phone. Reception upstairs is sketchy."

I do not smile as I thank him and move to find this Royce guy. The office is nearly black, but as we enter I can hear Royce saying good-bye to someone.

"Royce? Colonel David Gibson. I just came from the Command Center at Logan. We're wondering what gives."

It's only "we're" if you count Christina, but Royce doesn't know that. The man looks at me bug-eyed. He is sweating and breathing heavy and in a general state of pissed off.

"What gives? I'll tell you what gives. I have been telling these bozos for years to get a backup power supply to this building. Get something besides the transformer over in Watertown to keep this thing working. It's stupid to have all this gear and stuff dependent on one single power source not even located in the same city."

He grabs a handkerchief out of his pocket and wipes his

forehead. I hope he can tell me what I need to know before he falls over dead.

"But what do I know? I'll tell you what I *do* know. I know the lights are out in the Command Center. We could go shopping at Filene's or eat at Pier 4. They have power. But can we get a call in to 911? No. What do I know? I know the power is out. I know the radios won't work. The elevators won't work. We've got nothing. That's what I know."

He eyes Christina, which only seems to agitate him more.

"Who are you again? Who sent you?"

"Colonel David Gibson. Ms. Marchetti is with Senator Kerrigan. You are right and more of these idiots should have listened, but right now they need help. I need your help and I am listening. Tell me exactly where this transformer is."

He waves his hand at a map on the wall behind him.

"It's between Hunt Street and the Pike over off Exit Seven. Can't miss it. There will be twenty National Grid trucks all around the thing by now. But, hey! What the hell can you do?"

And we wonder how secrets get passed. I am not in the government, have shown no ID and we are in the middle of at least a hijacking and a power failure, and this clown up and gives me the keys to the kingdom.

I can hear him mumbling as we walk out. By the time we're walking past the kid at the front desk, he is yelling again.

The Caddy is still on the sidewalk and Tommy McKenna is looking none too pleased. I nod at him as I climb in while putting my high-speed satellite phone to my ear. A guy who used to work for me is now in the National Military Command Center in Washington, D.C. Mark is a watch officer, holding this job until he and/or the Army decides what his next job will be. I learn that the Pentagon has a rough picture of what is going on but was not aware of the communications shutdown, but I guess that's the point of a communications shutdown.

He was already inside the car talking. The car door now had a smug look. It was taunting me. Maybe if I tried being nice to it. I waited for the beep signaling it was unlocked and then gently pulled on the handle. Nothing. I tugged hard. It didn't notice I was there. I put both hands on the handle and yanked. It opened and I went careening back and landed flat on my ass.

I got up, brushed the dirt from my backside and got in.

I pulled the door closed behind me. It sat there innocently, as if it had done nothing. I stared at it, and then gave it the finger.

GIBSON

Everything happening tonight would strain the resolve and capabilities of the finest operatives the good guys have. So far we've had hijackings, a communications hub silenced, a disappearing natural gas tanker in the harbor, and, let us not forget, a U.S. military base on U.S. soil taken down. I need a SEAL or Delta Force or James goddamn Bond at my side, and instead I have a woman who can't open a car door without it turning into a one-woman Three Stooges routine.

She does not belong in this. I know that, but I'm not willing to let her go now. She has connections. She can help me. And . . . she's here. Doing her best. I don't have the SEALs, Delta Force or Sean Connery. I have her, and the way things are going, I will need a lot of help. I am not sure when it happened, but she has gone from being a wiseass, good-looking woman, way out of my league, to an operational asset. This fact should be telling me just how desperate I am.

I need to get to Watertown, now. I need to see if the transformer has been intentionally taken out, or if it is just broken. Broken is possible, but not likely.

I drive more slowly than I want through traffic and under city Christmas lights to get to the Mass Pike heading west. Now that I'm on the Pike, the Caddy can hum. I had the engine governor taken off so I can get this truck over a hundred miles per hour and get where I am going now, not later. The real trick is getting all the computers in these babies to cooperate. That was two thousand illegal dollars well worth spending.

We hit a hundred and ten. I push around to the right of traffic and into the breakdown lane. I let the weight of the car make the move, less wheel, more momentum. I keep my foot off the brakes and use the engine.

I had barely noticed when we hit eighty-five miles per hour. I was becoming numb to the whole speed factor. I heard the insane voice in my head. It was laughing a maniacal little cackle. *Ha ha ha! I laugh in the face of danger!*

Yeah, right! That's me.

When we hit a hundred and ten the voice stopped and all I could hear was my heartbeat.

The snow and rain were replaced by the December cold. The night sky was clearing. The stars were touching the ocean; the moon was half full, draping the city. If you took the time to notice, it was a beautiful night. We were not noticing.

It was at the end of the 135-mile Massachusetts Turnpike, a few thousand feet of six-lane highway that passed underneath the tallest building in New England, the Prudential Center. The Prudential Tunnel was completed in 1965 after years of political fighting; six lanes, three going east, three going west. It had withstood mad winter snows and floods. When it was built terrorism was not an issue. There was not a construction plan or thought that even considered what was happening now.

Suddenly there was a flash and heat. I could see fire all around the SUV. The whole world stuttered and seemed to move in slow motion. My body was thrown forward and caught against the seat belt. The force was so strong my teeth rattled.

My ears were filled with noise. It sounded like a speeding freight train—grinding, twisting metal and falling rocks. The car was flying through the air and stuff was crashing down all around us.

SECTION V

The battlefield is a scene of constant chaos.
The winner will be the one who controls that chaos,
both his own and the enemy's.

—NAPOLEON BONAPARTE

GIBSON

I am just clearing the tunnel, coming out from under the Prudential building, when I see the flash. There is a deafening
noise and the back end of my SUV leaves the road and we are
blown forward. I can see flames around us and I know we have
been hit by the blast wave of a BFE—big fucking explosion.

All the driving schools and crash-and-bang courses I've
been through are paying off. I relax my grip on the wheel and
steer into the movement; no brakes. It is like driving on ice,
but different. I get the car under control and do not stop. I look
back to see smoke and fire and cars turned every which way
but straight.

We need to get clear of whatever it is that did this.

The rear wheels slammed down and the truck careened to the right, heading for the barrier. We are going to die! flashed through my head in big neon letters. I stared with awe and terror as the concrete came closer.

Again, I could hear my mother's voice. She was talking about underwear. If I lived through this I really was going to need medication to stop the voices.

When I was a kid my mother would always remind us about holey underwear. Not holy, like blessed by the Pope, but holey—the kind with holes in it. She would tell us to make sure our underwear didn't have any holes in it. When we'd ask why, she'd say, "What if you got into an accident and had to go to the hospital?" It seemed unfair that other people who were facing certain death had their whole lives flash before their eyes, and my brain had to get stuck on which pair of panties I put on this morning.

I looked over at David. His jaw was set and he seemed in control. His hands were loose on the steering wheel as he maneuvered the car. He never slowed. He just kept driving away from the fire.

When we were three hundred yards from the tunnel, he pulled over. Thoughts were tumbling through my brain. What the hell was that? Oh, my God! We're not dead. I wore the purple panties—no holes. There were other people in the tunnel, are they dead? They're probably dead. Could anyone have survived?

I turned to look back and saw fire shoot out of the eastbound tunnel. A second later a car flew out completely engulfed in flames. Then the car veered to the left. Then, just as abruptly, jerked to the right. It flipped over and over and over again, and then skidded down the highway on its roof.

The noise reached us, and although it wasn't as loud as when we were in the tunnel, it was still deafening. The ground beneath us shook.

I sat gaping at the burning wreckage. There were people in there: families with little kids, and grandparents, newlyweds and . . . just people. Some of them had to be alive. You heard all the time about people surviving disasters. We had to try to help them.

I was trying to form words to tell David we had to go back when he flipped the car around. His tires screeched in protest. We started back toward the tunnel.

After the second explosion, from the eastbound tunnel, we cover the three hundred yards back so fast I barely notice. I slide the car sideways in front of the opening.

It is total devastation. Cars are blown apart, wheels are melting on pavement and concrete from the ceiling of the tunnel is all over the place. There are body parts stuck to the metal of what used to be cars.

No one is going anywhere for a very long time. There will be a lot of dead and very hurt people inside that tunnel, and the emergency phones are down.

We have to go in. No choice. Anyone still alive will be dead before the official help can get here. The fumes from the fire are toxic. Breathing them for only a few minutes can do serious damage. If the fumes don't get the people in there, the heat will. Fire contained in a tunnel burns hotter because it is confined, compressed air. In a matter of minutes it will be too hot to approach the entrance. Never mind, just get inside.

I unbuckle and look over at Christina.

"Any way I can convince you to stay here?"

She shakes her head no and unbuckles her seat belt.

"I didn't think so."

I can see determination and fear in her face. Good. At least she has enough sense to be afraid.

If I leave her here and she goes in on her own, she could get lost, or hurt, and I wouldn't know. Better she's with me. At least I can keep an eye on her.

I climb over my seat and reach back. I pull down the back-seat so I can get at the storage compartment from this end. Duke was right. It is a good idea to have two ways of getting at stuff.

"Chris, we have to cover up. Stay low in a crouch. The tunnel will act like a big funnel. The stuff can't go up or down, so it will be flying through the air straight at us." Wind, debris, body parts.

I sort through the stuff in the back. I put on my black work coveralls and a jacket from Carhartt. It's heavy-duty and might protect me from some of the fire. I throw Christina the gas mask and raincoat. It will have to do. It is all I have. We both get hats, gloves and ski goggles. I put the tactical vest back on and fill it with my personal gear: knives, pliers, gun in the holster. It takes only a few seconds to suit up.

I grab my aid bag and a flashlight.

"Chris, keep your hand on my left hip until we see what we are dealing with. Do exactly as I tell you."

4

MARCHETTI

I studied the gas mask. College had not prepared me for this. Not one of the classes I had taken involved dressing for chemical warfare. I pulled the straps because that seemed like a good place to start.

I was probably going to look like the creature from the deep in this getup. I was trying not to be vain, but I didn't want to die looking stupid. I had a great aunt who died while sitting on the toilet. That was the only thing anyone ever said about her since. A whole lifetime of experiences wiped away just because she looked stupid when she died. Just thinking about it made my heart rate jump.

GIBSON

She has the raincoat on and is working on the mask. I reach over and help her.

"Relax your breathing," I tell her.

She does it. I can hear her slow it down.

"The air is going to be really thick in there. Stay low, on your hands and knees. Try to stay below the smoke. It will take a while for the tunnel to clear, but we can't wait that long. The people in there need help now. Maybe we can buy them some time until the EMS gets here."

I don't say, *If they are not all dead.* We will know soon enough.

I can hear sirens now. I can hear a helo coming in too. It is probably WBZ-TV or some other news channel. One minute they are watching traffic, and now this.

"You sure you are up for this?"

I wanted to say that I was pretty sure I wasn't up for it, but I couldn't talk and concentrate on breathing. Breathing won out.

"I will need your help in there."

David Gibson didn't really need anybody's help, least of all mine, unless he planned on running for political office.

"If we are going to do any good, we have to go in there now."

I said a silent prayer and nodded. He tied a scarf over his nose and mouth and turned toward the tunnel. I reached out and put my hand on his hip.

GIBSON

The smell hits me first: burning flesh, melting metal and scorched rubber meet us before we are even inside. Then come the heat and wind.

We move into the tunnel maybe three feet, just past the entrance. I stop, crouch and listen. Chris does the same. I scan low to the ground looking for any movement, for anything alive. I can hear music. Someone's radio is still playing. Somewhere a cell phone is ringing. It isn't Chris's or mine. It is horrific and unexplainable what you will find that will survive a disaster.

I take out a whistle and start blowing, stop, then listen to see if anyone yells. Nothing. I blow the whistle again. No one responds.

Farther inside the tunnel, fire reaches the gas tank on a Chrysler minivan. The explosion picks the van straight up in the air. As it comes down, it blows apart. More crap flying through the air.

Best guess? No one survived in here. It is time to go. We will go and check the eastbound side, but I suspect the result will probably be the same.

I turn back toward the entrance. The news helicopter is four hundred yards back but only about one hundred feet off the ground. It is maneuvering closer, trying to get a better angle for the camera. They are filming the eastbound side of the tunnel. Time to get out of here.

MARCHETTI

I followed him out. I couldn't take it anymore. Being in the tunnel had been overwhelming. I had forgotten to breathe and then, to make up for it, I breathed too fast, and now I couldn't breathe at all and I wanted the damn mask off. We hit the outside and I ripped it off my head. I gasped, searching for fresh air and immediately started coughing. The smell was awful—gasoline, smoke, something that smelled like rotten eggs, and underneath it all, burning flesh and hair.

I followed David over the guardrail, heard the helicopter and looked up. Two people were inside. There was a guy with a video camera on his shoulder filming us. I could almost hear the anchorman's voice, *Want to know what these two are doing? Tune in at eleven and we'll show you our exclusive footage.*

I wanted to run, and probably would have taken off down the highway and run as far away as I could get, except something shoved me—hard—and I was on the ground again. First my face was pressed against the metal of the guardrail, and then David was on top of me, covering me with his body.

9

An RPG just took out the WBZ-TV news helicopter.

When things get blown up, pieces of those things fly at speeds only dreamed about by NASCAR fans. It is like an F5 tornado; ordinary things become missiles.

MARCHETTI

At first I didn't realize what was happening. Why was he holding me down? I just wanted him to get off me! I was about to tell him to do just that when I turned my head and saw what was left of the heli-copter fall out of the sky.

GIBSON

Chris and I are huddled between the side of the eastbound tunnel and the guardrail. I was offering up my body to be hit first. What a brilliant idea. With all your training, David, that is the best move you can think of?

When pieces of helicopter stop falling from the sky, I get up slowly, checking for any body parts that might have been hit. As always, I check my groin first. I ask Christina if she's okay. Dumb question, but have to ask it.

MARCHETTI

I looked over at David, who appeared to be making sure all his body parts were accounted for.

Okay? Was I okay? Ahhh, nope. I was definitely not okay. I gave myself a quick once-over and didn't see any blood. Again a voice in my head spoke up, but this time it was my old soccer coach saying, "No blood, no sympathy." So I nodded that I was, in fact, okay.

GIBSON

13

As I straighten up, I hit my head on a piece of metal. Part of the rotary blade from the helo is stuck into the concrete tunnel wall, inches from my head. I look around; a human arm is draped over the guardrail.

We need to get to my truck. We need to do that now and we need to do that fast. I look over at Christina. I can't tell if she has seen the arm or not.

14

Flames from the still-burning wreckage gave off enough light so that I could see the total destruction.

It reminded me of all those bad movies they made in the eighties about nuclear war and the end of the world. Everything smoldered and there were a few pops and crackles, but no voices. We could have been the last two people on earth.

David quickly looked all around, taking in everything. His eyes held half a second longer on a spot on the guardrail. I looked over to see what it was.

It was an arm. It had been severed somewhere between the shoulder and the elbow, and it hung over the guardrail. I couldn't stop staring even though I wanted to. Male. Left. The hand still had a wedding ring. I waited for someone to yell *Cut* and to come over and pick up the plastic prop. No one did. Then I waited for it to move on its own. That didn't happen either.

His name had been something like Jeff or maybe Hank. Some financial job in the city made him commute on the Pike to his house in the suburbs. He had twins, a boy and a girl, with a pretty blond wife who adored him. It all played out in front of my mind. Good God, they had just spent Christmas together and now the holiday would be . . .

David said something, but he sounded really far away. Then he leaned down next to me, grabbed my hand and talked into my ear. I turned to look at him, still not understanding what he had said. There was smoke all around us, and noise I couldn't identify. He looked impatient, ready to move. Apparently I was holding up the show. I snatched my hand away from him and got up.

"We need to move."

She's moving like she's swimming in molasses and unaware of anything going on around us. Shock. I want to blame her, but I cannot. I want to shield her, but I cannot do that either.

Two state police cruisers are heading toward us, followed by ambulances and fire trucks. They are coming down the Pike, fast. There is a loud bang, and the passenger-side window of the lead police car is shot out. The car swerves to the right. The car behind tries to avoid a collision. It doesn't make it. The car flips.

The ambulances and fire trucks look like they are taking rounds from someplace high up and to our left. Boston is a war zone.

MARCHETTI

David pushed me down and my arms flew up over my head.

I'm not sure where women get their survival instincts, but there is probably a good reason why we are always portrayed as running through the woods toward the cliff in high heels. It's because we would do it. With me, there's a fifty-fifty chance I'd be doing it barefoot, but otherwise, yeah. The only thing that might save me is I would probably trip before I made it all the way to the cliff.

I brought my hands down and looked around. David was crouched next to me.

"What the hell is going on?"

Oh, I don't know, it could be a post-Christmas celebration or it could be violence, mayhem and the total absence of happy thoughts.

"Someone is shooting at us," I say.

"At us?"

"Possibly just near us, but to be safe let's assume at us."

The first shot had been aimed at the police car's window. The burst that came next was all over the place. The bullets were piercing the engines of the vehicles. They must be using black-tipped ammunition. All of this makes sense, from a certain twisted point of view. If you shoot at the first responders, then the next group of cops and firemen who show up will be slower and more cautious. People who need help will have to wait. More confusion, fear and death added to an already chaotic environment. Can't wait to meet these guys. Can't wait.

I grab her hand again and pull her behind me. I need to find a way to get us clear of whoever is doing the shooting. We hug the wall to our left and, using the mangled state police cars to cover us, we cross over. We climb back over the guardrail and haul ass to my truck.

I lurched after him. My feet were slipping and catching on all kinds of stuff. I did not look down. If I was tripping over a human head or sliding through guts, I didn't want to know.

We reached the car and I scrambled in. I had no trouble with the door this time. It was that adrenaline thing. "Mother Lifts Two-Ton Car off Baby." Christina Marchetti opens bulletproof door. Same principle.

GIBSON

I get radios and binos from the back compartment and switch back to the M4 with the 14.5-inch barrel. I put four extra thirty-round magazines in the Paraclete Level IV ballistic vest along with some grenades, both the smoke and antipersonnel types. The vest will stop handgun rounds pretty consistently and some long gun rounds. They will leave marks and hurt like hell, but that particular pain is a reminder you're alive.

I take the monocular for myself. I hand a radio and binoculars to her. I double-check the Safariland 6004 thigh rig dropleg holster and the four-inch Spyderco pocket, folding knife with the serrated edge. I really did not have any idea what I was heading into, which made me want to take every single thing in the car with me, but that wasn't feasible.

I start the car and take off. I'm going to the closest exit off the Pike and away from this kill zone. The assholes doing the shooting have made few mistakes, but they have made some. First of all, they are shooting bursts. Bursts make lots of noise and give off quite a signal. Second, they picked apartments that were nice and close to the targets on the Pike, which also makes them easy to spot. I think I have a pretty good fix on their location. We have got to get to them before they pull up stakes. We have to get to them before they realize that they are now being hunted.

"What are those?"

Well, they are not candy! I swallow my annoyance at the distracting questions.

"Grenades."

"Oh, good."

No, very bad for whomever gets them.

20

MARCHETTI

The man carried grenades in his car; the same car he drove at a hundred and ten miles per hour. Also, the car he did his grocery shopping in and took through the McDonald's drive-through.

This car was driving someplace and I didn't know where. So far, my track record with these kinds of trips was pretty bad.

GIBSON

I can't keep running around like this. I'm good, but no one is that good. I am going to need some help.

I pick up my cell phone and dial.

"Duke? David. You heard about the shit up here?"

"Yup."

"Well, there's more shit than that. A lot more, more than I currently have time to explain. I will tell you this: Marge is on the plane."

"David . . ."

"Thanks. Look, I need you, Neil, Fast Eddie and Lou here, now. I am quickly running out of airspeed and altitude. Call when you are en route."

"You know I love your mom, man. She doesn't deserve this, after having you as a son. We'll be on our way in under an hour."

Duke really cares about my family. More importantly right now, he can really help. When you are in combat with someone, you become bonded by blood, fear, joy and misery. Duke and the rest of these guys and I have been in the shit together and survived. When I was a young lieutenant, they all saved my butt from stupidity, and later I saved them from disaster. We are living now because of each other.

"Duke, check our sources. Get the best intel update you can, but don't slow down getting that info. Pay whatever you have to pay, I will cover it. Duke, bring everything."

So we can add Duke and Fast Eddie to Fuller Brush Man. For a man who won't use contractions, he sure loves nicknames. I was going to want something better than "Legs" by the time this was over.

Given what David had in the back of his car, I wondered what was included in the "everything" Duke was bringing. Tactical nuclear weapon, death star, or something fudge ripple?

He tossed me a walkie-talkie-looking thing and a pair of binoculars.

"This is a radio. These are binoculars."

The condescending male thing pissed me off, under the circumstances. I gave him a doe-eyed look and said in a really breathy Marilyn Monroe voice, "Gee, what does this button do?"

"Yeah, okay, be a wiseass, but in about three minutes you are going to need to know how to use them. So, you want to listen or you want to bust my ass? It's completely your choice."

I actually wasn't sure what the button did, so I was quiet.

"The guys shooting at the cops and firemen—that's an ambush. Usually, when you set up an ambush, you expect the enemy to turn around and run away."

"Well, sure. Wait, we're not doing what they expect, are we? That sane thing. Running away?"

He went on as if I hadn't spoken. "By attacking straight into an ambush you do two things: you surprise them; and you put rounds into those who are shooting at you before they put rounds into you."

"We're driving toward them, aren't we?"

"We are going to attack the ambush site."

"These are the guys who shot a helicopter out of the sky, right?"

"Listen, the cops are great, but they will never be able to act quick enough. There is too much going on all at the same time."

He showed me how to use the radio, and then we checked to make sure the radios were working. I had a sudden urge to have a code name and say things like *The* Eagle *has landed,* but I didn't mention it. This wasn't sixth grade, and I wasn't with my friend Bridget stalking Ryan Smith to see whether or not he was meeting Gina "the Tramp" for ice cream. I was sitting in the middle of a war zone with a guy with a big gun who was about to go after certifiable bad guys.

Most of me had the common sense to be petrified. Part of me was excited. Even I don't understand women.

SECTION VI

Guilt is perhaps the most painful companion of death.

—Coco Chanel

GIBSON

We take the Copley Square exit, hang a hard right and get within two blocks of Boylston Street. We are moving to the 1500 block, where I saw the shots come from. Chris will act as my spotter.

"Grab the wheel. I will slow down. When I jump out, you pull the truck over and keep me in sight as best you can."

I take her left hand and put it on the wheel.

"You are my eyes and ears. I need you to pay attention while I am out there. I have to be able to count on you, so if you can't handle this, now would be a great time to tell me. I am going into that building to stop whoever is shooting."

"I am your eyes and ears. You're my big gun."

That sounded dirtier than I'd intended.

"This is important. I need to know if you see anything that even looks like police. There can be no mistakes. Only bad guys die from now on. "

I unlock the door.

"These assholes who did all this should have been watching. If they were watching, there is a good chance they will recognize the car. They won't know what our story is yet, but they might decide they don't want to wait to find out. The car is armored, so you will be safe."

I open the door and put my left foot on the running board.

"Chris, don't panic. Just let the car roll forward until you can get over into this seat. Then start looking."

I grab my M4 that is wedged between the seat and the center

console, turn on my night-vision goggles and step out the door into the abyss.

For some reason, a picture of my mom and dad watching me play hockey flashes in front of me. I think it was a good moment. Mom was always yelling and Dad was always embarrassed that she was yelling.

Shit! I hit the curb too hard, stumble and roll. Not a pretty movie exit, but nothing is broken. This hijacking thing with my mom on board is really affecting my concentration and focus. I'll feel more myself when I kill something.

MARCHETTI

I heard myself scream as he stepped out of the door. Before today, I couldn't remember the last time I'd screamed when it didn't involve a bug or a horror movie. This was starting to annoy me. I made a mental note to try to stop it while I scrambled over into the driver's seat.

I looked in the rearview mirror just in time to see David roll on the grass, get up and start walking.

What was with the walking? We couldn't stop long enough for him to get out of the car, but now he has the time to go for a stroll? He probably jumped out just to scare me. It worked.

My mind clicked. Two things we had recently said fell into place. They shot a helicopter out of the sky. You'll be safe. Only one of those two sentences could be true.

I pulled the car over, closed the door and brought the binoculars up to my eyes. I located David and then scanned over toward the apartments looking for bad guys, but I wasn't entirely sure what they would look like. Would they twirl mustaches and laugh in a sinister way? Would they wear uniforms with a big BG on them so I'd instantly know the bad guys? I thought about calling David, but I could already hear his answer without him saying it: *They're the ones shooting at us.*

GIBSON

Walk normal. Don't run or duck, don't move at angles; look like the rest of humanity out here. Slouch a bit, not too straight. Blend.

I have the M4 under the work jacket with a double sling, nice and secure. I am only using the night vision when I have to. There are plenty of lights here in Boston near BU. I move in a direct line toward the football field and a large apartment building.

"Chris? This is Dave. Over."

Nothing.

"Chris? This is Dave. Over."

Why isn't she answering?

MARCHETTI

When I looked back to where I thought David should be, he wasn't there. I scanned around, figuring he couldn't have gotten that far, but I still couldn't find him. Suddenly a voice broke the silence in the car and I jumped, hit my head on the roof and screamed. So much for curbing the screaming thing.

It took me a second to realize that the voice was David on the radio. I snatched the radio up and promptly dropped it down by the gas pedal. I reached down to get it and couldn't reach it because I had closed the raincoat I was still wearing in the door. I pulled harder trying to free myself, but no dice. I wasn't thrilled with the idea of opening the door, since people had been shooting at us earlier. So instead I wiggled out of the coat. This time when I reached for the radio I got it. I sat up fast, knocking my head into the steering wheel.

"Shit."

I pressed the button on the radio and yelled, "What do you want?"

5

"What I want is not the point. That you answer me the first damn time all the damn time is the point. My ass and yours are on the line, so pay real close attention. Can you see me now?"

"Ah, no. You disappeared."

"Turn the car around and drive slowly to the corner. Take a right and get to the highest point on Comm Ave. Then look for me. I will signal you. I am going to start hunting now, and you are going to help me spot."

Can't get more stupid or desperate than this: a politician as my spotter. When Duke and the boys get here this whole thing will get better. I just hope I'm alive to see it.

I hear my truck before I see it. I pull out the Streamlight flashlight. I hit the button twice.

"Chris, this is David, did you see that?"

6

I put the radio and binoculars on the passenger seat and drove around to Comm Ave. I was ready to start hunting bad guys. Except now, on top of really needing an IV bag full of coffee, I had to pee.

"Sort of."

I hadn't seen it, but I didn't want to admit that. I was busy looking at the road where I was driving this goddamned humongous tank.

"Chris? This is David. Pull the car over to the right shoulder, stop and look to your right."

Okay. I didn't really think that he had to tell me who he was. Who else would be on the radio calling me by name? If someone started speaking Arabic into the radio, I think I'd pretty much guess it wasn't him. Well, hell, maybe he spoke Arabic too.

I pulled over and looked to my right. I saw a light flash twice.

"The flashlight. Sure, I see it."

"Good. Now, as best as I can, I will use this light to let you know where I am, by flashing it twice. Any more than that and the bad guys might see it.

"I need you to describe things to me relative to my position."

I wasn't exactly sure what he meant by that, but I figured yelling, *Look out! He's right behind you!* was pretty close. I really hoped I wouldn't have to say that.

I move down the street close to the buildings I suspect the assholes are shooting from. This would be the logical choice, since this is the highest spot the shooters could have used, unless they are better than I think they are. Most anyone can hit anything from five hundred yards or closer, especially with the optics available today. God, it's me, David. I won't swear anymore, I'll promise you anything, but for a change, give us a break.

This is a nice section of Boston. It paints a pretty picture: mostly college kids, but a few middle-income families. It feels like it's usually a comfortable place.

WHACK! CRACK!

The bad guys are still shooting at the cops. The cops are now shooting back. This should help distract them.

"Chris, this is David. Where are the shots coming from?"

There is another gunshot and her voice comes over the radio.

"Fifth floor, fourth window in."

Good woman, she really is a quick study. I pick up my pace but notice that there is a van with no windows. Engine is on.

Occasionally, in Special Forces, you get to go to schools with the CIA. Before I went back to Bosnia, I was allowed to go to "the Farm," where detection and observation courses were taught. You don't need to be an expert to know that vehicles running in the middle of the night without windows during a terrorist attack fit right in there as something that needs to be detected and observed. I stop to get a closer look. The van has a satellite antenna on the roof. Okay, no more observation needed.

Chris is coming up in the truck.

"Chris. David. I am moving to my right thirty yards in front of you. There is a van six cars up from you on the right that looks dirty. I am going to check it out."

I took the binoculars away from my eyes and looked for the van. I found it. It really wasn't all that far from me.

Suddenly there was a sound like popcorn popping, but muffled. The air in the car compressed and it sounded like it was raining rocks on the car. Next thing I knew, David was shouting over the radio that people were shooting at me and that I should drive the truck into the white van.

I live in Boston, before that it was Providence, training grounds for the worst drivers in the world. I have often fantasized about driving my car through the trunk of some asshole that cut me off or ramming some ninety-three-year-old lady who was crawling along the highway at three miles per hour. I understand road rage. I've mastered it.

I was feeling something just a little more than road rage right now. These people were shooting at me.

I stepped on the gas, cut hard to the right and the truck ate the driver's side of the van.

The impact was jarring and I smacked my forehead on the steering wheel. Lights danced before my eyes.

The guys in that van just shot up my car. Sounds like an AK-47; a full clip. Chris is in direct-fire danger; her only way out, her only weapon, is the Cadillac. I hope she has the guts to do what has to be done.

The cold night air makes the sounds sharper. The twenty-two-inch all-weather tires grab the snow- and ice-covered alley street. The 6.2-liter five-hundred-plus-horsepower engine has a dull, deep-throated roar to it when you stomp on the accelerator pedal, and Ms. Marchetti is definitely stomping on the accelerator.

I watch my Cadillac destroy the van. The extra two thousand pounds of metal and ceramic plating have helped make the already heavy vehicle act more like a tank than a car: it also explains why Christina has been having such a hard time with the doors. Well, now, she can ram a truck very nicely. I would not want to be on the driver's side of that.

I come up on the back of the van and move around to the passenger side, staying low. I stand and fire through the passenger window and shoot the guy in the passenger seat through the side of his head. I get down again. I move around to the front and fire through the windshield, hitting the two assholes in the back. They take two rounds each, one in the head and one in the chest. I check the driver. Chris killed him on impact.

These were probably not the guys shooting at the cops on the Pike; those guys are probably still upstairs. These were the guys who hurt my car. They were only guards or lookouts. Actually, now they are neither.

I make my way to my car.

"Are you okay?"

I open the door and she stumbles out.

"*Why* do you only ask me if I'm okay when you *know* I'm not?"

"Yes, you are. You did great. Nice driving. Great reaction. The driver was killed on impact. I got the rest of them."

She stares at me for a second and then takes a swing at me.

I catch her fist in my hand and gently ease her arm down. Give her credit. It was a nice try.

"Feel better now? Look, these guys are connected to the people that blew up that tunnel and probably to the people holding your mother and my sister. Killing them was a good thing."

She blanches at that. Killing being a good thing isn't an easy concept.

"I have to go into the apartment and take care of the guys still shooting at the Pike. Put your gloves on; cover your mouth and nose and eyes. Then go through this van and these guys' pockets.

There are police and fire siren sounds everywhere, but the rest of the area is quiet. We are not seeing anyone even curious yet. That will change quickly, and it will make our getting out of here more complicated.

"I am not putting all that crap back on. No way."

"Hey, ever heard of AIDS? Infections? Nasty things? Just cover up before you go into the van. Take anything with writing on it. Take cell phones, computers, pagers—anything that looks important. Stay on the radio. I will be back in ten minutes. If I'm not, drive away and get help."

She nods. She's got this wild-eyed look to her.

Killed on impact. I had killed the driver. I couldn't just go around believing David had shot them all. I had killed the driver.

That had to be wrong. I couldn't have killed him. I couldn't even kill a spider, not since I saw *Charlotte's Web*. Oh, my God! I had killed him.

My stomach turned over.

I am a lifelong member of the Democratic Party. I was a Democrat in my mother's very Catholic womb. We don't advocate killing. We most certainly don't ever say it is a good thing.

Maybe, I thought, people like me take that position because we don't want to be the ones to do it, even when it is necessary. No, Chris, not now. Later. I would figure it all out later. Right now didn't seem to be the time for moral reflection and introspection. I swallowed the urge to retch and tried to focus on what David was telling me. I was surprised that he was still talking.

"You did the right thing. You saved your life and mine. Thanks, by the way."

He walked away. I waited until I couldn't see him anymore, then I bent over and threw up.

GIBSON

Good thing I had the air bags disconnected or she would be really pissed and have an even wilder headache.

Simple redbrick apartment buildings with concrete foundations and steps built between 1940 and 1959. From August to May, it's a crowded neighborhood when the college students are in. The buildings all have flat roofs and cluttered porches where the students sit and drink. The streets are made for smaller cars than what we have today. A typical northeastern city neighborhood, this could have been in NYC, Philly or Jersey. At this time of night and this time of year, no one is around.

The night quiet is broken by alarms, yelling, police radios and bullhorns from the explosion site, sirens from fire, police and ambulances responding to what has just happened; an exploding tunnel tends to draw attention. The site we just left is only three hundred yards straight from where I am standing but a mile-plus by car. The distinctive sound of 5.56 shots coming from the apartment building next to me. Whoever is shooting should have been long gone by now, which means they are very stupid or committed to dying; either way will not be good for them. The frozen snow pops as I move toward the apartment. I am checking my gear as I move.

I have to get to the fifth floor, fast. I walk past the elevators and through the emergency exit door. I start up, two stairs at a time, my M4 pointing up. The place seems almost deserted. That's a good thing.

The door says fifth floor. This building is at least eighty years old and has thin doors and walls. A radio is playing in one apartment and I remind myself that some students have probably stayed here through the break.

I count down to the fourth door, putting out the lights in the ceiling with the butt of my M4. Maybe they will hear me and come out—that would be nice—or maybe they'll hear me and get nervous. Strange popping and shattering glass sounds in the hallway might unhinge those with the guns—that would not be nice. Anyway, this is the way it's playing out today. Lights would mean I would be silhouetted in the doorframe. Can't have that.

I listen at the door first, then reach into the back pocket of my vest, grab my stethoscope, and listen again. I hear Arabic and Serbo-Croatian. It is time to move. I shoot three rounds into the upper and lower door hinges, and then three into the lock. Wood chips fly.

I kick the door open, pull the pin on the M 84 stun grenade and throw it in the center of the room. Wait for the quick bright light and explosion, then blow through the doorway following the smoke from my stun grenade; move quickly to the right corner because I am right-handed and it is open. A guy with a gun, standing back from the balcony but shaky, turns and I double-tap him in the center of his chest. He drops down to his knees and falls forward on his face.

There is another guy sitting at a table using phone books to prop and steady the sniper rifle. He is grabbing his head, still dizzy. He is now turning his rifle and his body toward me. I roll to my left, fire and he flies back, out and over the balcony. I stay down.

There is a third guy, coming from the kitchen area; from his angle he cannot see me. He comes in shooting wild in all directions, screaming. He is making a lot of noise. I wait until he is past me, then take him with two to the back.

I keep the M4 up and ready, deep in my shoulder. I slide across the floor, crossing my feet but not lifting them. We are trained to do this, to be always in a shooting position, especially after a shoot-out. Expect the unexpected type of thing. Your heart is pumping. You have just killed somebody. The feeling can be distracting if you let it, and distractions can get you killed.

I look the dead guys over quickly. Small holes where the bullets went in, larger holes where they came out. Blood flowing out of the wounds and across the floor. Eyes open, mouths in grimaces, signs of pain; not like sleeping, a lot like dying violently.

I quickly check all the rooms. All gone. All dead. Gone to Terrorist Hell.

I clean the apartment. Lingo for check for stuff that will tell me what has happened here. I take out my Sony digital S35 and take pictures, videos and voice notes. I love this little camera.

There is not much: a two-day-old *Boston Herald*, pizza boxes, Coke cans. They've been here a couple of days. There are no papers on these guys, just two computers and a cell phone. I take them with me.

Their prayer rugs are out.

I never get this. Lives devoted to prayer and terror. Pray five times a day, then go and murder children. I am more than willing to help you get to your heaven sooner than later.

I hope you all got your last hypocritical prayers in today. On second thought, I hope not.

I stood there retching for a few seconds; then tried deep breathing. It didn't help. When all else fails, move forward. Do something. I hurried over to the van, opened the passenger-side door and looked in.

Four dead guys. Eyes wide, bleeding from various places. Glass everywhere. My stomach rolled over again. I stepped back. No way was I going in there. I cursed David and paced back and forth.

I heard gunshots coming from somewhere and realized it probably wasn't a good idea to be standing in quite so open an area. If I wanted to die, I probably could have just waved and yelled, *Hey! Over here. Shoot me.* Trouble was, I didn't really want to die.

I was muttering all kinds of things that would curl the hair on a Hells Angel. When I ran out of conventional phrases, I started making up new ones. I pulled the gloves out of my pockets and put them on. I pulled the goggles down over my eyes. There was no way I was putting the gas mask back on, so I decided if I actually had to get in the van, I would try to breathe as little as possible.

When I get really nervous, I sing. In high school and college I belonged to the school theater groups. Before every performance, they'd find me sitting somewhere alone, singing. On Election Day, I am a virtual karaoke machine. It's hard to totally freak out when you are trying to remember the words to "Copacabana" or "The Piña Colada Song." It's also hard to sing when you have to hold your breath because you won't wear the gas mask.

Humming would have to do.

I brushed some of the glass off the dead guy in the passenger seat and started humming "The Rainbow Connection." I was totally creeped out, so naturally I thought of Kermit the Frog.

There was a small hole in his right temple and the left side of his head was completely missing. I had never seen a real bullet wound before. No matter how good the special effects guys get, nothing in a movie could ever be as bad as this.

I felt through the front pockets of the guy in the passenger seat and found nothing. Then I slid my hands under his ass and felt in the back ones. Nothing. One down, three to go.

There wasn't any way to get at the guy in the driver's seat through the driver's-side door. David's truck was still pressed into the door and even if I moved it, there was too much damage; I probably wouldn't have been able to open it.

I walked around to the back and tried the doors. They were locked.

Shit! Shit! Shit! I could feel tears stinging my eyes. I stamped my foot.

Get a grip.

". . . Someday we'll find it, the rainbow connection, the lovers, the dreamers, and me . . ."

I was going to have to either drag the guy out of the van's passenger seat or climb over him. Since sitting in some dead guy's lap wasn't high on my list of things that I ever wanted to do, I walked back and hauled him out. He hit the sidewalk with a heavy wet thwack.

I stepped over him and climbed in the van. The driver was slumped over the steering wheel. The seat and terrorist number two had something I strongly suspected was Sidewalk Guy's brains splattered on them. I hummed louder and pushed him back in the seat. His eyes were open. He looked surprised.

Don't think about it. Just check his pockets and get out of here, I told myself. Tears were rolling down my face, but I stuck my hand in his right front pocket, then the back right one. The left ones were harder. The door was pushed in and I had to move him again to get into them. When I did I found more nothing.

Now I was pissed. If I had to feel dead guys all over, the least God could do was put something in their pockets. I climbed into the back of the van. There was shattered glass everywhere.

I was actually more than pissed. I was enraged. I hated these guys. I hated them, and for half a second I hated everyone like them. It was completely irrational and not as uncomfortable as I would have liked and it was true. It was easy.

I scrambled into the back but found nothing there either. No papers, no pagers, nothing that David had said to look for. I scurried back to the front seat and was backing my way out the passenger door when I saw a cell phone down by the gas pedal. I leaned over to grab it and had to put my head in the guy's lap to reach it. I wrapped my hand around it and jumped out of the van.

I took off my gloves, dropped them on the ground and did an I'm-creeped-out dance, which basically involved me jumping up and down, shaking my head and hands and making *blech* noises. I ran my hands through my hair. I could take a lot, but stuff stuck in the hair would definitely push me over the edge.

I shook the cooties off me, finished my song in a loud voice and headed back to the truck. I climbed in and heard David over the radio telling me to start the car. He was on his way out. I would wait for him. I was proud of myself for finding the cell phone, and if I left him behind there would be no one to tell. He probably thought I couldn't take it; that I hadn't done what he'd told me to.

After all that had happened, there was no way I was prepared to wear the wimp label. If nothing else, David Gibson was going to learn that I was one tough cookie.

Now all I had to do was convince myself.

SECTION VII

It's only half past the point of oblivion,
the hourglass on the table,
the walk before the run,
the breath before the kiss and
the fear before the flames,
have you ever felt this way?

—PINK

I

GIBSON

I wasn't 100 percent sure she would still be here waiting for me. I climb in the passenger side and she hands me a cell phone. She looks almost impressed with herself, but just below that is fear and a million other emotions.

"Are you surprised you are still here? Before you answer, let me tell you, I am not."

She turns and jabs her finger into my chest.

"You're damn lucky I'm still here. I could have left, you know. In the time it took you to . . . to do your thing, I could have made it back to my apartment, showered and crawled into bed. I could be in my bed right now with the covers over my head, trying to forget all of this."

She sniffles. I hope she is not going to cry. I really, really hope she is not going to cry. I will be lost, undone. Innocents crying remind me of my mother when she is upset. The Gibson men are weak-kneed around whimpering women. It would certainly be true with this woman. If she goes and does the vulnerability thing, I will come unglued.

"You did real good back there, and I would love to pin a medal or something on you, but right now, Chris, you need to drive."

She backs the car away from the van and flinches at the sound of grinding metal.

"Drive straight and slow. Make sure you stop at all the lights. We don't want to draw attention to this shot-up, semicrumpled thing of beauty. With all that is going on in this city, less attention is better. Speed draws attention. Running red lights draws attention. We've already done enough of that for a while. I am going to call Fuller and arrange to get him the computers and phones we found. He really is not going to believe this shit."

She drives and I swear she is humming something the cast of Glee would turn down for being too kitschy. I pull out my phone and dial Fuller.

"Hey, Mark, I have—"

He is practically screaming at me, asking me if I know what the hell happened on the Mass Pike.

"Yes, Christina and I were there. Slow down and let me back-brief you."

I tell him what went down, how many we killed, what we found and that I will bring it all to him as soon as we are able to get there.

"Colonel, you killed seven people, saved some of my guys' lives at the Mass Pike and have evidence on what is going on in and around Boston. You are kind of a hot property right now. Where exactly are you?"

"We are on our way. Marchetti is Superwoman. I mean it, Mark, she attacked the ambush as if we had trained her ourselves. Now tell me what is happening with the boat, and how is the plane with my mother?"

2

He told me to drive while he called Fuller, but he never said where to go. I drove to my apartment.

There was a limit to what I could take. I had reached it. The rest of the world, Fuller, my sister and terrorists included, were just going to have to wait. I was going home to pee.

I pulled into an empty parking spot out front and turned off the car. David was still on the phone with Fuller. I hauled my bag and body out of the car, fished around for my keys and ran up the front steps of the restored tenement.

As I unlocked the door, I waited to hear the truck pull out and drive off. I wasn't sure if I cared if he did or not. I opened the door, flipped on the hallway lights and climbed the stairs to my second-floor apartment. Once inside, I bolted for the bathroom.

Splashing water on my face didn't change the fact that I looked like hell. I walked back into the kitchen, dumped coffee and water into the coffeepot and turned it on.

My apartment looked the same as it had when I'd left it this morning, even though everything else in the world had changed. It was comfy and homey. I took a breath and realized how tired I was, how dirty I felt.

I climbed on my knees on an overstuffed couch to peer out the front window. The truck was there. It looked like David was still on the phone. Screw him. He was on his own now. I was done.

I walked back to the bathroom, turned the shower to scald and stripped off my clothes. They were covered in stuff I didn't want to recognize or remember, so I threw them all in the trash. Nothing from today was salvageable.

I stood under the water and scrubbed until my skin was raw. Then I did it again. I washed my hair and did the conditioner thing. Then I closed my eyes and let the water pound on my forehead. I saw pictures of the plane, the Fox News alert, flashes of the guys in the van—eyes wide open, bleeding. I could hear gunfire and explosions. I could hear and see everything, but all I could smell was the soap. I breathed deep.

Crying is something I don't do, or at least don't admit to. Aside from it being girly and weak and it making your eyes red and your face puffy, it means you are out of control. Genetics, environmental programming and my career choice don't allow for out of control. Today, the world seemed out of control. Today, out of control seemed appropriate, the rational decision.

If I could have, I would have stayed in the shower forever and had myself a good cry, but in my apartment twelve minutes of hot water was all you got and I was thirty seconds away from being cryogenically preserved. I shut it off and got out.

The sight in the mirror was no better than a few minutes ago. I had purple welts on my arms, scrapes on my knees, a cut on my face, a bruise in the middle of my forehead—and that was just the front of me. I'd save looking at my backside for tomorrow's entertainment. I grabbed my robe from behind the door. It was the pretty emerald-green silk one I got for my birthday. I threw it on, tied the sash and followed the heavenly scent of coffee into the kitchen.

David was sitting at my table.

GIBSON

3

People who do what I do aren't inhuman, however much they wish it were otherwise. They still need food and bathrooms and even appreciate showers once a week or so. Sitting at a simple kitchen table, smelling coffee, breathing slowly, these things can help refocus you, let you see the big picture. I haven't been able to put this all together yet, but for the moment I feel a little bit more in control.

I hear the water turn off and watch as she comes into the kitchen. If she is surprised to see me, she doesn't let on. She just moves to the cupboard, takes down two coffee cups and pours.

"Black?" she asks me.

I nod.

She looks like maybe she has been crying.

She hands me the cup and leans back against the counter. The wet red hair drips beads of water down her neck. The robe is tied, fitting all the right places. She is a distraction I cannot afford.

"Chris, look. Nice place, but we need to be officially out of here."

I stand and walk toward her.

"I'm not going anywhere," she says.

"Chris, how about you lose the contrary, stubborn, wise-ass reflexes for a moment and listen. Fuller knows your name. We have just been involved in seven homicides and the biggest terrorist attack on this country since 9/11, which makes our homes the first places the good guys will come looking for us. And they will come looking fast."

"And why don't I want the good guys looking for me?"

"Because they will arrest you and throw away the keys. In case you have forgotten, we have just killed people. In Boston. In the middle of a terrorist incident. Hell, they may not be sure they can trust us."

Her eyes get wide as what I said sinks in. "But . . ."

"People have died. Our families are in danger. If it matters, I am very impressed by the way you handled yourself."

I reach out and touch her hair. She looks up at me with this trusting, needy look. She's strong, but trembling.

I want to grab her and kiss her hard, I want to know if right now she has the same need that is almost overwhelming me. I want her hands on me; I want her to want my hands on her. She smells of soap. Time to stop, before stopping isn't an option. I take her hands and turn them palm up and kiss her hands, with as much tenderness as my life will allow. There is a war on all around us, that war pushed us here, it is probably the only reason we are together and that fact is enough reason to stop.

I push her away gently, but keep my hands on her hips.

I take a deep breath and look at her hair while avoiding her eyes, "Go . . . go get dressed. We need to get out of here."

She leaves the room, I assume in search of clothes. At least most of me hopes she has gone to get dressed; the stupid, thinking-with-the-wrong-part-of-my-body part . . . hopes she is not.

4

MARCHETTI

All along I knew that I couldn't stay at the apartment. The fact that I could experience some legal trouble had not escaped me, but I really wasn't in the mood to make things easy. I was thinking that just once he was going to have to do things on my terms. Sometimes I just can't get out of my own way.

I grabbed black jeans, a turtleneck and a sweatshirt and slammed the closet door. It wasn't as if the whole thing would have taken up a whole lot of time. I grabbed underwear out of the drawer, checked for holes and slammed the drawer. I'd killed today and wasn't about to take any guff from a closet or drawer.

When this was all over, I would look up what *guff* was. I should know what it is if I'm not going to take any of it.

5

My cell rings.

"Gibson? We're here."

"Duke, where the hell is the *here* you're talking about?"

"I met Fast Eddie in Manchester. Lou met us at his car dealership in Lowell. Neil is driving up from the Cape. I need to tell him where to meet us. We need to get in as few cars as possible, transfer all the toys and get this show on the road. So, my young apprentice, what now?"

"Okay, how about we meet at the old MDC Police Station at the beginning of Storrow?"

"You mean the place we staged for the hijacking training?" Duke asks.

"Yup. We need to brief you guys. We need to have Neil look at these cell phones, then we have to get this stuff to Fuller."

"I told Neil to bring his equipment. All his phone detection and electronic testing gear is down to the size of a PalmPilot. Even looks like a PalmPilot. He can always call in a favor from the National Security Agency if we need to. Neil says if it is in the air, the NSA can grab it. Now, see, I think that is a scary thought, but—"

I'm afraid of one of Duke's tangents. He works for the government, but you couldn't say he trusts them. He's not alone in our line of work. "How soon can you be there?"

"Depends on the traffic getting into the city after all this. The Pike is closed. I'll figure it out and let you know ETA as it becomes clearer."

MARCHETTI

6

I rummaged around under the bed for my boots—ones that would keep my feet warm and that I could actually walk in.

I wasn't sure what the almost-kiss was about or if I wanted a repeat of it, but I was going to show him what he missed out on. I was going to run around on this crazy wild-goose chase. I was going to be brave and competent and useful. I was not going to scream or cry or throw my hands over my head; or at least I wasn't going to do those things a whole lot. I was going to help save my sister, the free world and stick it to David Gibson all in one fell swoop.

GIBSON

I have a lot of rules in life and I think I had just broken two-thirds of them with the almost-kiss. All in all, probably not worth it. It was just adrenaline, that's all. Don't make it anything more than that. People as complex and different as Christina Marchetti and David Gibson are not meant to be; the universe is way too complicated and orderly to allow such nonsense.

She walks out of the bedroom with her hair pulled back and dressed in black. She has a serious don't-screw-with-me look on her face. She has more attitude than common sense. I need to get her out of this, for her sake and mine.

"Chris, about the . . . thing . . . my fault. I must be getting old or tired or both. It was completely my fault. I apologize."

"You came in here because . . . ?"

"Now, can I have my keys?"

8

I felt some disappointment. So he wasn't here because he wanted me to go with him or because he wanted me. I nodded and went looking for them.

Most people would just walk away from this, but I had started something and would finish it. I would prove myself to him and to myself.

Damn straight it was completely his fault.

I pitched his keys at his head and he caught them easily. My father always said I threw like a girl. Guess he was right. I locked up and we got in the car.

I make the engine turn over and we are off.

"What now?" she asks as she puts the seat belt on.

"I need to meet some people. You are going someplace where you will be safe and not in my way."

"So tell me about this Duke guy you called."

Her voice is quiet and firm as she ignores what I said.

"Yeah, this Duke guy is the reason I went into the Special Forces. Friend of the family. He is five-foot-eight and 250 pounds wide. He has a face that looks like it has been pushed in by a baseball bat. Actually, it has been, almost. He is smart, experienced and snakelike-quick.

"He has done more killing for this country in more places than most people have traveled. He is also one of the kindest men I have ever known. He knows explosives, communications, weapons. Hell, he is a weapon . . .

"He'll like you, but he is harmless. Well, maybe not harmless, but he won't do anything while I am around. I think."

"Who are the others?"

"Lou Foserelli is just tough and smart. He's hard as nails, having grown up in Haverhill. Going into the military saved him. Was a cop, has more money than God; knows more about cars than anyone should; and can shoot good enough to be on an Olympic team. He is dark, Italian, handsome. He will like you too."

"Terrific."

"Neil Doig is the best damn medic and communications

guy who ever lived, and Fast Eddie can hit a gnat's ass from a thousand yards away all day long and has forgotten more about terrorists than I will ever know. We have fought together and survived. I trust each and every one of these guys with my life and now I trust them with yours."

"I'm sure your friends are all very nice—"

I cut her glib sentence in half.

"No, they are not very nice. None of us is the kind of guy you want to take to a movie, or even be seen with in public, but when it gets bad, I mean blood-in-your-eyes, crapping-in-your-pants, they-have-my-children bad . . . these are the only people you ever want to know. After that, put us all back in a box and drop us off a cliff. We understand and we kind of like it that way. We are all 'Break Glass' kind of guys."

"Break Glass in Case of Emergency?"

"Yes. We all live in that dark place that people like you are fascinated with, but you don't want to go there, not even for a visit."

10

I listened while David told me about his friends or associates or partners in crime; whatever they were. He said more about them than he had said about anything all day.

It ran through my head that whatever kind of lives these guys had had, they were probably very different from mine. David measured everything in terms of life and death. Up until today, those kinds of thoughts hardly ever crossed my mind. His world sounded very exciting and very lonely. It also sounded like life expectancy wasn't a real hot topic of conversation.

David sounded a little relieved that we were meeting them, which was good. He also sounded a little more determined, which I thought might be a bad thing.

I was just as scared as I had been before.

After he finished telling me about the boys, I was out of harmless questions that wouldn't lead us to trying to one-up or kill each other. We were driving, sharing a not-so-comfortable silence. In fact, it was a downright tension-filled, uncomfortable-as-hell silence. He hadn't mentioned the safe-place-to-stow-me again and I needed to keep him away from that line of thinking.

SECTION VIII

There is something about killing people at close range that is excruciating. It's bound to try a man's soul.

—Steven Spielberg

I

GIBSON

After we hit the second detour sign, I get it. The Boston PD has correctly decided to funnel all the traffic in and around Boston to where the cops can check it, control it and stop it if they need to. Considering what has happened at Logan Airport and under the Prudential Center, it is a very good idea; unless, of course, you are trying to get somewhere fast, then the idea really sucks.

I look over at Chris and do the eyebrow-raising and frown. I have got to get this now-slightly-less-than-perfect Cadillac Escalade, with a little extra and some slightly illegal gear in the back, through all this obstruction before I can get back over to Storrow Drive and to the old Metropolitan District Commission Police Station where the boys will be waiting.

We are detoured around the back streets of Boston with at least six turns and pull up to a checkpoint. We exit the car at the request of the officers, who are dressed like they are going off to war. I try the ID thing, but no dice. They are intent on searching the vehicle. When they find the stuff in the back, we will be done. I'll be explaining and filling out forms forever, at least after they let me out of a cell.

Chris moves over beside me and suddenly it's old home week.

The older cops are looking and talking to her like she's their daughter, the younger ones are looking at her like she's lunch. She throws me a look that I can't quite read, but I think she is telling me to back off and let her handle it.

"Okay, which one of you guys is in charge tonight?"

"That'd be me, Christina."

A cop who had been standing off to the side moves forward. She looks a little taken aback.

"Hey, Mac." Her voice is softer than before.

"Hey, yourself."

There is a pause and I am thinking that I don't have time for this.

"What are you doing out? The world's coming to an end right now. It's not safe out here," says the new friend, this "Mac."

"I heard. We need to get somewhere."

"Your apartment is in the other direction, so I know you aren't headed home. Where are you going, Christina?"

The guy's tone, the way he's looking at me and the fact that he knows where she lives says it all. He's the ex. From the look of things, I'm guessing it wasn't him that ended it.

"It's a long story."

"Always is with you, Chris."

She moves to take her cell phone from her bag and the ex just shakes his head.

"The magic cell phone trick won't work with me, Chris. Your senator has no authority over me today."

"Fine. Then you make the call, but I want you to call Major Mark Fuller. This gentleman can give you the number. Do you know who he is?"

"Of course I do." The look on his face has changed.

I give him the phone number, although I was sure Mark had given her his number. She moves over to two policemen and has them move the sawhorse. I'm not sure how. She walks back and signals for me to get in the Caddy while her ex is trying to reach Fuller.

"Drive. Now."

"What did you say to those cops?"

"I told them Mac wanted them to move the sawhorse."

"Hoo boy."

We cruise into the four-lane, brightly lit, smooth-walled Big Dig tunnel.

"You realize you will never speak warmly with him again? And your friends on the cops will probably never trust you again either."

"I know. I didn't see an option and we didn't have time to be creative or wade through phone calls. I did what we had to, but I didn't enjoy it."

"For what's worth, I don't see any better way either, and . . ."

It's a damn miracle, this tunnel. Built under Boston Harbor for more than $22 billion, it is the most expensive highway project in the history of the United States. It rerouted the existing Interstate 93, which was the main route through the city, into a 3.5-mile tunnel. The project also included the construction of the Ted Williams Tunnel extending Interstate 90 to Logan International Airport, the Leonard P. Zakim Bunker Hill Memorial Bridge over the Charles River and the Rose Kennedy Greenway in the space vacated by the previous I-93 elevated roadway. The tunnel runs a few feet to a few hundred feet below the surface of the harbor. The pressure of an ocean pushes in on you as you drive through.

It all happens at the same time. The car slides forward, not under my control. Debris flies past us from behind, followed by a ball of fire and behind it a wall of water.

We are being pushed forward, chased by heat and water. Whatever happened in back of us is allowing the harbor into the tunnel at an enormous rate. The added weight of the armor on the car is the only thing keeping us stable.

I do not have time to tell Chris anything. I can see the Storrow Drive exit to our right and I struggle to force the car in that direction. The exit ramps up and should help keep us ahead of the water for a moment. I look at Chris and . . . Who the hell could she be calling now? I don't ask, as I am trying to keep the car from being swallowed up and spit out.

MARCHETTI

Maybe it was everything about today and the fact that I had already survived one tunnel being blown up, but I knew what was happening before I could really see it or hear it. Something had made the tunnel give way.

When we were kids and we'd go through one of the older tunnels in Boston, I'd hold my breath and look for leaks. This was more than a leak. It was a big hole, and I could see the Atlantic Ocean rushing in at us.

The last time a tunnel blew, the cops and firemen had come screaming in and someone had shot at them. It seemed logical that they would do the same thing this time. My brain processed it all and I grabbed for my phone and dialed Fuller's number.

"Ms. Marchetti, I just got a call from a Boston policeman and—"

"The tunnel is blown."

"Got that covered, emergency personnel have already been into the tunnel—"

"Not that tunnel. The Big Dig."

Silence.

"You have to stop the cops and firemen from showing up here."

The car swerved as water hit the side of the car; I grabbed on to the dashboard and almost dropped the phone.

"Why would I do that?"

"If they show up outside the tunnel, there will be people shooting at them again."

David was steering toward the exit, trying to beat the water out of the tunnel. He managed to pull out of the tunnel as water pushed us into a barrier.

3

GIBSON

The tires spin, fight for purchase and finally grab. The SUV begins to pull away from the rushing water and I veer over onto the exit ramp, climbing up and out of the tunnel. I take one second to marvel that we're still alive, but only one. I pull the SUV over and onto the curb.

"We need to do a look-see. Can't let what happened at the Pru happen again," I say as I get to the back of the truck and pull out the M4, Second Chance vest and SIG. I make a quick check of the gear while I put it on. I turn my cell off and throw it in the box.

I think she is yelling at me; but I am moving too fast to even tell her to stay put.

A couple of dirty white trailers sit up against curbs, swallowed by the shadows of tall buildings. It's a construction site but I can't even tell what they're building. A railing rims a steep drop down to the rest of the construction site. There is sand everywhere—some to make the roads easier to drive, some from the concrete mixers running 24/7. Dirty snow completes the scene, making everything a dingy gray. The police blockades in the city are starting to take effect and the streets seem deserted. Temporary construction fences line the site and seem to attract storage bins, trash cans, Porta-Potties, even some large and small front-end loaders.

I scan the area. There are at least six places where they might have set up to hit the first responders. The first of which is a trailer by a construction site in front of me about twenty yards away.

I move toward the trailer, and a homeless man holds a half-gloved hand out to me from a cardboard box. Right now I am hunting and don't have time to help.

"Sorry, brother. I'll be back to take care of you."

I turn to look him in the eye so as not to insult him. He is holding a shotgun. Two quick shots and I am blown back. I dimly hear a third shot and I am tumbling over the railing. I am floating, and then the world turns black.

"*No!*" I screamed, and dropped the phone. There was a roaring in my ears, and fear and panic flooded my brain. Oh, my God! He's dead! The man with the gun walked to the guardrail and peered over. Rage replaced the fear.

I was over the seat and into the storage compartment and then I was opening the door and running. I had a gun in my hand. I was thirty feet away when he lifted the gun and aimed down over the side where David had fallen.

Suddenly the air was filled with a bloodcurdling scream. It was my voice. The man turned and brought the gun up and aimed it at me. I was still screaming as I raised my arms, pointed and pulled the trigger.

The gun jumped wildly, but I kept shooting. By mere luck one of the shots hit the man in the head and he crumpled to the ground. I fired until the gun was empty. The screaming stopped, but had been replaced by crying. I dropped the gun and ran over to the guardrail.

I looked over, even though I knew what I'd see. David was lying motionless, faceup, on the ground.

I turned away. I was shaking so bad that I had to sit down, and when I did my hand touched the shotgun lying next to the dead guy. The guy I had just killed. That made two.

I heard a door open and looked up and saw a man come out of a trailer that was parked on the side of the road. He had a gun. He called out in a language I didn't understand. He didn't sound happy. When no one answered, he left the doorway and moved toward me.

I slowly picked up the shotgun and pointed it at him. He was moving closer but still didn't see me. I tried to control my breathing and remember not to sniffle. He was ten feet away and the slight rise of the road and sidewalk hid me from his view. He did not see me yet; but it would be only seconds before he did.

I was scared and angry and sad and a million other things. I knew this guy would kill me, just like the other one had killed David.

I had killed one man accidentally with a truck. I had shot one man wildly out of fear and anger; this one was going to be on purpose. This one was going to be revenge.

The man moved closer and I lifted the gun, aimed it as best I could, which, since he was almost right on top of me, didn't take much. I took a deep breath and pulled the trigger. The kick made the gun fly out of my hands. I scrambled after it. He fell over.

That made number three. Minutes passed, but no one else came charging out of the trailer. I just sat there clutching the gun for a while, waiting for anybody else to show up. A weird calm settled over me. The shaking had stopped and my breathing was slow and even.

Eventually, the do-something feeling overcame what had to be numbness. I laid the gun down and got to my feet. There was a construction ladder to my right that led down to the site and David. I hauled myself over the guardrail and climbed down.

In the movies, people feel for a pulse. In real life, you stand in a nursing home or hospital and wait for the person to stop breathing. They breathe out, you breathe in and hold it and wait for them to take the next one. Eventually you get light-headed and realize they aren't going to do that. I looked at David's chest. It rose. Holy crap! He was alive.

I scurried over to him and put my hand on his chest. Yup. Breathing. Relief washed over me and was instantly replaced by the now-what? feeling.

His arms and legs weren't twisted funny nor was his head bleeding. He had been lucky with that fall, well, as lucky as a man who had just been shot could be said to be. I unbuttoned his vest, which was covered in small holes and burn marks. Underneath it there was another vest thinner and tighter than the first with more little holes in it. It was ripped. I undid the Velcro straps. His chest was covered with red welts that had started to turn purple. They were all over his chest and stomach. I gingerly felt around for the gunshot wound I knew had to be there. Nothing.

Jesus Christ! Where was he shot?

"David?" I shook him a little. "David?"

No response.

"David, wake up."

Still nothing.

David's phone wasn't in one of his many pockets. Mine was on the floor of his car. There wasn't anything to do. He was alive. I'd take it. I'd wait for the police to show up. I reached out and found his hand.

I hear her before my eyes focus. She is crying. Shit, but my chest and stomach hurt. My back ain't feeling too good either. What the fuck? Got to get back in the fight, but first I have to wake up.

I open my eyes and see a tangle of curly red hair, and then red-rimmed, puffy green eyes that are staring at me with disbelief and relief.

"Who died?" I ask

"I thought it was you."

"Sorry, I got a little sidetracked there. I'll be okay in a minute."

I sit up slowly. And damn, but this hurts. I check the nads first, then the eyes, and then the less important bits. Everything present and accounted for. I blink a few times until I can focus. I look down and check out my chest: real sore, but no blood. I think I might rather be shot, and since my illustrious career has afforded me that particular experience five times—I can compare it. This is definitely worse. Falling thirty feet probably didn't help any.

"Are you okay?" she asks really softly.

"Better than you think but not as good as I'd like. Did I miss anything?" I ask her, not really sure how long I have been out.

"Someone shot you. You fell down here. I shot the guy that shot you and then I shot his friend."

She tries for matter-of-fact, but I can hear the quaver in her voice. I check to see if any of my gear is missing while I drink some water and take some Aleve to mitigate the pain that I know is coming. I find my M4 next to me, must have kept hold of it longer than I thought. I reattach my chest protector. It saved my ass this time, but I will not be doing any bathing suit modeling for a while, too many welts. Time to go. I take my M4 and use it as a crutch. I get my right leg under me, then my left.

"Chris, we need to get out of this hole, back to the car and then out of here, and we need to do this now. The cops are not going to be happy."

The cops are going to want an explanation. Don't care if she is the Pope's niece, no amount of connected is going to let us walk away from this. The trick would be to be gone without leaving a trace, which of course is impossible unless we are going to bury the bodies or take them with us. I guess we could stash them here, but it would take too much time. We are screwed. We need to go.

"Hey, how did you get down here? Fly?"

She rolls her eyes and looks completely exasperated. "Nope, I left my Batgirl cape at home. I came down the ladder."

She points to the construction ladder. Thank God there is a ladder. She goes up first, I am right behind her.

Each rung is real pain; I have to use too much arm because my legs are still not cooperating as they should, and this pulls on my chest, which is screaming. The pieces of what happened are coming back. I remember the homeless guy. There was a shotgun. I sort of remember falling. The sweat is pouring off me. I need to focus on now.

Chris screams and I look up. We are close to the top and someone has reached over and pulled her up and over by her hair. Obviously they missed seeing me, or I'd be dead. I was having too much trouble climbing and was a few rungs behind. Time to overcome my injuries and save the damsel.

One more rung and I grab the rail, which runs along the top of the concrete barrier. I pull myself over but stay low, hugging the top of the barrier. The idea being to give whoever is up here as small a shooting target as possible.

I see Chris and two assholes; both are dark-skinned. Got to be Moroccan or Algerian. One is skinny and slimy-looking; the other is stocky, about 220 pounds and somewhere under six feet. The big one is pulling her backward. She's got her hands in her hair trying to lessen the pressure. She is swearing like a longshoreman.

I come up with the M4. This shot is going to be tricky. The big guy is holding Chris in front of his body. No clean shot for me, and I'm hardly 100 percent. The red dot from my aiming point is not steady. I need to close the distance between us. They are moving toward the RV. Still no clean shot, and almost no room to maneuver. More importantly, there is no time to do anything to make sure I don't hit Chris. I need to hit this guy just right so I do enough damage so that he can't shoot back. I'll take the slimy one out first. He is closer. They both turn toward the trailer. I push my breath down to my stomach, breathe out slowly and my vision becomes a tunnel with a slimy Arab at the end of it. Right then he turns to check behind him. I can see his face clearly.

"Hi. How you doing?"

I put two fast-moving 5.56 slugs through his chest. He falls back toward Bulky Arab, and I actually see the blood come out of his back. I am within five feet of Bulky Hair-Pulling Arab, and as he quickly looks at his friend, I put two rounds in his left shoulder.

This is not television or the movies. When you get shot with a bullet that moves as fast as a 5.56 it hurts and you react. Hair-Pulling Arab lets Chris go and she falls on her back. I step over her and put two more rounds in his back as he tries to run toward the RV. He was yelling something in Arabic, but I silence him. He falls to the ground twenty yards from the trailer.

I turn back to Chris, who is still on the ground, holding her head.

"Get your ass back to the SUV; things are about to get even uglier." She gets up and moves . She actually followed directions.

One clown sticks his head out the door and I get off five or six rounds at him but miss and he's back inside. I take out my

Randall handmade survival knife, wedge it through the latch, so the door can't be opened. I move quickly to the front of the RV. I hear the engine start to turn over; they are trying to get away. I squat down in front, sling my M4 over my back and reach into my left inside stow pocket for the prerigged grenades.

By pulling the pin and wrapping two rubber bands around the handle you make each grenade easier to use. It's dangerous but quick.

I pull the bands off with my thumb, hold two grenades in my right hand, count one . . . two . . . open the door . . . three, toss both inside the RV and close the door. There is the bang, and then the door flies back at me with considerable force. Sounds of screaming fill my ears as I enter the front door amid the smoke, broken furniture and shattered glass.

I shoot two rounds at what was once the driver. He is slumped over on his side, half on the floor, half still in the oversized driver's chair. I turn to the left and see four more men in various stages of dying, all with parts of their bodies missing. Two grenades at very close range will do that. I shoot the first guy twice in the chest. The second one has a laptop carrying case—the shiny ones that can be reinforced—in his lap; both his hands are missing. He gets two rounds in his chest cavity. The two remaining men in the back are dead. I take the laptop case and throw it toward the front door. One more check for anything that might tell us more about who these guys are . . . Nothing.

I go out the front door, walk to the back and recover the Randall. My father gave it to me years ago and its rightful place is in my vest, not being used as a door lock.

I make my way back to Chris, who is sitting on the floor in front of the passenger seat. She has six feet of body squished into a four-foot space and looks halfway to shock and the rest of the way to exhaustion. I look over at her and smile. "So, are we even now?"

6

MARCHETTI

David helped me up into the passenger seat. He changed the magazine in his gun.

"Are you okay?" he asked.

I looked over at him. "We're not dead."

"And I, for one, say this is a good thing."

"How come we're not dead?" My words sound far away.

"Are you complaining?"

Okay. The funny-guy routine wasn't funny. He was making jokes and I wanted him to stop. Before today, I had never even held a gun. What had I been thinking? I had grabbed a gun, not knowing how to use it, not knowing if it was loaded. Church was now going to be a requirement in my life, either as a thank-you for the miracle that allowed one of the bullets to actually hit the bad guy—although that seemed somehow wrong—or as penance for the whole thou-shall-not-murder thingy.

My entire head, inside and out, hurt and I probably had a big bald spot from the guy pulling me by my hair. There were lots of things I could handle, but being bald wasn't one of them. The uncontrollable, can't-see, can't-breathe, shoulder-shaking sobbing thing hit without warning.

He touched the side of my face with the back of his hand. I leaned into it and covered his hand with mine. We sat there for half a second. I spent two and a half minutes devoted to self-pity and then it subsided. I wiped my eyes with my hands and tried to breathe.

"So what does this mean? Are we going steady?" He smiled.

"You can either be nice to me or we can go do something hard. We can't do both. So what's next, Colonel? Where to?"

SECTION IX

All God does is watch us and kill us when we get boring. We must never be boring.

—CHUCK PALAHNIUK

GIBSON

"We need to get to Duke and the boys."

I can see blue lights in the rearview mirror. For a few minutes, I'm nervous about them seeing us, but they don't follow. I feel her looking at me.

"Talk to me. Tell me things. About you and the boys."

I turn to her. "Listen, you have killed three people today. You did it to save yourself and me, and it was the right thing to do. Eventually you are going to have to deal with it. I can crack jokes and talk about anything you want, but it won't change it. At the end of all of this, you will still have killed them."

She shrugs.

"Tell you things. Okay."

I adopt my lecturing colonel tone.

"You are about to meet four of the most deadly human beings on the planet. The boys and I were together on the same Special Forces team in Colombia, Afghanistan, Yemen, Morocco, Bosnia and Kosovo and other parts of the unpleasant world.

"We all walked away from the military when our bosses refused to let us do our jobs. Because they wouldn't let us do our jobs, an entire town full of men and boys in Bosnia was wiped out. Over eight thousand men and boys were killed and we could have stopped it, but no one in the chain of command had the balls. We all own part of the responsibility for what happened there and we live with it. I could have stopped the killing, or at least made the Serbs pay. Fast Eddie had the murdering asshole Lieutenant General Ratko Mladic, aka 'the Rat Man,' who was running the roundup, in his sights for over an hour and we were ordered not to shoot.

"I should have taken the rifle and done it myself. I chickened out. I should have disobeyed the orders yelled at me over the SATCOM radio link, both from Stuttgart, Germany, the Special Forces headquarters, and from NATO headquarters in Mons, Belgium. They all kept saying, 'Stay out of this. Just report. It is not what it seems.'

"Goddamn it! I let those people die.

"I will never stand by and do nothing again. I had never before laid down and have not since, but on that day I was a coward.

"I have never told that story to anyone. I don't think I will do it again.

"When we decided to make out a report on what we saw and how we saw it . . . well, let us just say the Army made the next five years rather interesting for us. I was quoted in a paper saying something about how governments can be cowardly. It was an election year, kind of strike three for the Army and me. The boys backed me up all the way and they suffered for it.

"Anyway, after that I put my papers in. Then Neil, Duke, Fast Eddie and finally Lou followed.

"Now we do some private work together, sometimes for our government, sometimes for the money. We are each very good alone, but together we are even better. We get together when things are going very bad, and today things are going very bad, and it's probably going to get worse. We are very good at what we do."

"Why?"

Her voice is quiet and I almost miss the question. I have never been any good at talking about what makes me tick. I have not talked this way with a woman like this. Out of the corner of my eye I can see her. Her head is down and her hands are clasped in her lap. I realize she is asking why we choose to do this. Not an easy question.

"We are different. We are really not any smarter or any tougher than anybody else. What separates us from the rest is our willingness to go in the door. Lots of people talk about it, lots of people think about it, but we know that each of us has and will again go into that dark place. We will go in and do what others cannot even think about."

"But why?" Her voice is louder and more insistent.

"We each started it for our own reasons. Duke was given a choice: he could either join the Army or go to jail. He was caught robbing a grocery store and the judge gave him a break. Lou joined because he came from a life of privilege and wanted fun and adventure. Fast Eddie because he was poor. Neil joined to get away from his dad, who was a preacher. I did it because my dad did it and to get revenge for my brother. In the end we stayed because we were good at it, we stayed for each other and we stayed because . . . we like it."

I wait for her to say something.

"But, why?"

Good goddamn!

"You ask too many questions."

"Actually, I've only asked one question. I've just asked it three times. I'm waiting for you to tell me the truth."

I should just shut up.

"If you press us for an answer we will tell you that we do it because of each other. We like knowing that we each can count on the other. We like knowing we can be counted on. You wind up loving each other.

"You love each other because you have held your friend's guts in your hands, put them back in his stomach, wrapped him up, then laughed about it later. You love each other because when you broke down and cried so hard you threw up from the fear, they did not laugh or ever remind you of it, as they too had been there. You really love them when they have the fresh chewing tobacco in the middle of a rainstorm in the backside of hell. You love them because they are the bravest, best men you have ever known and just being around them makes you feel better.

"I guess that is what we like, the feeling, not the killing. But the killing is part of it and you can't duck it."

I had asked him to talk to me because I didn't want to think about me killing people. So now I was thinking about him killing people. It had been hard for him to talk about and I wasn't really sure why he had. Some strange part of me even wanted to protect him, which seemed ridiculous, now that he was conscious and armed to the teeth.

I was amazed, but I actually understood how they could "like it." Today, on top of being the worst day of my life, had definitely been the most exciting. Most of me was busy feeling guilty, bruised and numb, but part of me liked knowing I could do it if I had to. It was a primitive survival instinct—something in the core of us we don't want to admit is there anymore.

Luckily, there was no more talking or self-exploration because we finally got to where we were going. We took a right into a parking lot and pulled around back and waited. Over the next forty-five minutes four cars would join us. There was hugging and backslapping and typical macho-guy hello stuff. I climbed out of the car to watch, fascinated.

The guy I figured was Fast Eddie was the first to arrive and didn't say anything, just leaned against his truck holding what looked like a machine gun. He was thin and wiry and looked like 170 pounds of tightly bound wire. His eyes were slightly slanted, almost Asian-looking. He didn't really look at me; he looked right through me.

Next to arrive, Lou was so typically Italian-looking, he could have played a starring role in any Mafia movie. He had dark slicked-back hair that framed a dark-skinned face and dark eyes. He glided more than walked and he threw me a you-want-me, I-know-it look and went about his business.

We sat around quietly waiting for the others. David wasn't going to brief anyone until the entire team was there. A truck pulled in and one of the largest humans I have ever seen climbed out. Neil was huge. His hands looked like they could bend steel, but he was quiet and calm. He had dark hair and dark eyes and a scar through his right eyebrow that made his face look interesting.

I studied them all; they ignored me. I had become wallpaper. No one acknowledged me until the guy I guessed was Duke arrived. He stared me down and let me know he was not happy.

Duke was shorter than me, but made up for it in muscle. He was all muscle and moved with astonishing grace. His face looked as if it had, over time, taken a beating. It was pushed-in in places and raised in others. His nose was crooked and skewed and had obviously been broken more than once. His eyes were hard and cold and his stare bored holes in the back of my head. I recognized the glare for what it was.

So what? Between my mother and David, I was used to the evil-eye thing. Plus, after today, I was a certified badass too. I held his gaze to let him know I wasn't intimidated—much.

"All right," I say.

Duke says, "Let's get the hugging out of the way, and save all the I-told-you-so's for later because we need to make some decisions now."

"Duke . . . Duke, you miscreant, I have been shot with a shotgun and thrown over a railing. Did I mention I was shot? So maybe we save the hugs for later, too."

I get a questioning look from Duke.

"I'll tell the story later; for now, I am okay."

They go about unloading and checking their gear. I catch Duke eyeing Chris, who is now standing beside me.

"This is Christina . . . and I know. I know what you're thinking about her and about me, but her sister is on the plane with my mother. She is okay and she is with me. She has managed to save my ass, kill three bad guys, manipulate the Boston Police Department and for grins deployed a platoon from Seal Team Two. She has earned the right to be here, so save the bullshit for later."

No one says anything out loud. Trunks on all four vehicles open.

"Neil, your 500SL may not look too pretty after all this is done, so let's take Lou's Suburban and my ride."

"Gibson, if there is so much as a bad look at my car, I am taking it out of your ass with interest."

"Little touchy 'bout the ride, are we not, young Louis?"

They start unloading black bags and putting them in the two trucks.

Duke walks to the trunk of his Caddy and I follow. I count four long guns: AK-47, M4, Remington pump sawed-off shotgun and an H&K sniper rifle; and six handguns: four .45-calibers and four nine-millimeters.

We all get used to the toys of the trade. The new stuff may be a bit lighter or have more gadgets, but unless you have a lot of time on your hands to retrain, sticking with what works for you is what you do in the Dark-Side-of-the-Force business. You really want a comfort with your tools.

Duke's got enough ammo and explosives to start or stop a small war. Det cord, timing fuses, wires, first-aid boxes, radios. All the stuff we need.

Duke is being Duke. Love him, but not now, my large, dangerous friend, not now. I watch while he tries to stare Chris down and she gives it right back without flinching. After a while I can tell he is impressed. Full-grown serial killers cower in front of Duke, but not Christina. When his look changes from menacing to lustful, hers goes from tough-guy to not-in-this-lifetime.

I step between them, hand Neil the phone and computer and give Duke the digital camera.

"Neil, can you check this computer out? It was a gift of some friends back on Storrow Drive. And Duke, stop breathing on Chris. She's saved my life twice and killed two bad guys in the process, so as of right now you are playing catch up to an untrained civilian woman.

"We have to get organized. I owe Fuller an explanation and there is no telling what the FBI will want—besides my ass, that is. Duke, download the data from that camera. Neil, let me know what you can about the phone. I'm taking suggestions for our next move." They usually have sound tactical advice laced with sarcasm.

"David," Lou says, "you have been carrying this fight for a while and been doing it pretty goddamn well. What do you think?"

"I think I need help. I've been running around from fire to fire and I want to get to the next fire before it's lit."

I turn and ask Neil what he thinks. He disconnects from the call he was on.

"I think you always talk too much. My friends in New Jersey tell me this cell phone was bought here in Boston with a stolen credit card. The memory has been erased but maybe our friends at Fort Meade can get something on this. Would take a couple of days."

"We don't have a couple of days."

"I figured."

Duke just mutters, "Your play."

Fast Eddie just spits some Red Man and shrugs. Fast never says much.

"Chris, what do you want to do?"

She looks kind of stunned that I asked her. Then she looks kind of pissed because I have put her on the spot.

"Whatever you think."

I say to the guys, "Chris and I have some real personal reasons for all this, and we have broken enough local, state and federal laws, starting with murder, to keep a roomful of asshole lawyers busy for a year. So we may be in some trouble. Even so, we have hard evidence that the good guys could use. I think we need to get over to Logan and get this info to Fuller, without getting arrested.

"Chris, how about your senator? Maybe you can call him and buy us some time before they throw away the key."

I don't want to owe her. I really hate asking for favors, but I don't have a choice now. There is just no way that I am going to waste my time arguing with lawyers or cops or both while my mother is in danger. Ain't going to happen.

"I'll try," she answers.

Lou's new Chevy Suburban and my newly marred Caddy get filled with distributed gear and we head to Logan and the F Troop Command Center.

4

I'd bet these guys looked scary sitting in church, even all decked out in their Sunday best. It was easier to imagine them sitting in a bar on a Friday night, drinking beer, looking normal, but the image wouldn't fine-tune. Besides, wherever they hung out on Friday nights—when they weren't busy invading small countries—was probably nowhere I had ever been. Part of me thought I'd like to go. The rest of me seriously considered having that part of me committed.

Calling *my* senator to see if he could make it so that we weren't arrested on sight seemed about as feasible as calling the Pope to see if I could get him to change his mind on the whole birth-control thing.

I had to try. We'd left about fifteen bodies in our wake, without counting what we'd found at the Coast Guard station. Since I hadn't brought my own bombs or guns, my connections were the only way I could be even slightly useful.

GIBSON

5

We have been at this for nine hours. Considering what we know and some things that we can guess, we have a well-trained, well-armed, superbly financed terrorist group operating in Boston. There are a lot of people smarter than I am seeing this and coming to the same conclusion.

This will be the first real-world counterterrorist operation of this scale on U.S. soil since 9/11. Everyone will be clamoring for his or her piece of the glory pie. The first group will be the FBI's Emergency Response

This bunch of staffers with radios and computers are all tightly wound by-the-book types who gather as much information as they can for other tightly wound by-the-book types. They'll come to Boston to be eyes and ears, but it's the brains in D.C. will make the decisions.

Next, along comes the Hostage Rescue Team. This is the nation's preeminent civilian SWAT team and is made up of the best and brightest the FBI has to offer.

Third in line but fighting for bureaucratic supremacy is the Department of Homeland Security Emergency Command Center. This group consists of everyone from the Coast Guard to the Federal Aviation Administration to the Treasury Department and so on. This is a tricky group because they, along with the FBI, have not had to deal with any real-world crisis. They have done simulations and security for the Salt Lake Winter Olympic Games, but there is nothing like the pressure of an actual crisis that needs resolution.

The next group will consist of representatives from the Joint Special Operations Command (JSOC). This is the staff and command for three groups with tactical teeth: Special Forces Operational Detachment, Delta Force, is the Army's best counterterrorist unit; SEAL Team 6, the Navy's equivalent; and Task Force 160, "The Night Stalkers," the world's best helicopter pilots. Combined, these three groups are the world's utmost killing machine.

Then, of course, the hangers-on will assemble. My bet is that over two thousand military, federal, state and local players will show. All will have their own support, communications, vehicles and command. All will want their chance to spill the bad boys' blood. There will probably even be a destroyer or two steaming nearby to help handle the tanker issue. Logan Airport will become, if it hasn't already, an armed camp.

We need to stay free. So far I have kept my own personal ghosts at bay. I don't even know how my mom is doing. She has buried two sons; one died in Somalia and one in a car accident. The FBI had better figure out what to do, and fast, or I will do what I can to reduce this situation to something controllable. I will do so by resuming killing people. I am uniquely qualified to assist. The boys have added to my ability to create mayhem by a factor of ten. For everyone's sake, I hope they get this right and we do not have to get involved. It gets very messy and requires lots of paperwork to clean up.

6

Lou, Fast Eddie and Neil got in the other car. Duke was sitting in the front seat of David's truck, looking menacing. I wrestled with the back door. It weighed the same as the front door, but without the attitude. I climbed into the backseat and placed the call to Kerrigan's office. Mary Katherine answered.

"It's Christina," I said, and waited for the verbal assault.

"Oh, my God! What is going on down there? The news has reports that there was an explosion under the Prudential Center and another one in the Big Dig and a *rumor* that there was a massacre at a Coast Guard station—of course, I know it's not a rumor. They are saying that some of the police and rescue workers were shot at. Fox News is reporting that something is going on with a supertanker . . . of course that hasn't been confirmed. The senator has been on the phone nonstop and hasn't told any of us anything. What is going on?"

"I really don't know."

It wasn't exactly a lie. I knew more than Mary Katherine, but I didn't really know what was going on. She didn't buy it.

"How can you not know? You are right there. I know you must know something. Michael called back, and let me tell you, he was not pleased with me. He wanted to know how I knew there were thirteen dead people at the Coast Guard station. Imagine how surprised I was to find out I knew that. I only knew that there had been a shooting. You left out some very important details, you know."

"Mary Katherine—"

"I want to know what is going on or I swear I'll tell him it was you that called me. You owe me."

There it was. I owed. If I wanted to talk to Senator Kerrigan and not have my ass thrown in jail, I was going to have to pay up. I tried to think of any piece of local gossip I had picked up that would trump a coordinated terrorist attack, but came up with zilch. It was Christmastime and all of the extramarital affairs had been put on hold for the holidays.

"Okay, but you have to keep it quiet."

"I will. I swear."

Uh-huh. Sure.

"The tunnel and shooting stories are true. I was there. The boat thing—"

"Oh, my God! You were there? . . . How . . ."

I waited until she finished yelling more questions at me.

When she came up for air, I said,

"The boat thing could be true, I don't know anything about it."

I hadn't really told her anything she didn't already know, but now she could say she had inside information.

"What is going on there?" I asked.

"Senator Kerrigan is beside himself. No one seems to be able to locate the President. The Secret Service has him in one of those secure, undisclosed locations. Ever since the word came down about what's been going on in Boston, he's been MIA.

"Kerrigan is furious. Called him a coward. Said he should be visible when the country is in crisis."

Maybe it was a valid criticism, but to the best of my knowledge Senator Kerrigan hadn't gotten on a train or in a car to head back to Boston. Unless he was going to grab a bucket and help dig people out of the rubble, I didn't think going forward with those accusations was a great idea.

"I think he is probably hiding out in Maine. You know, he was up at former President Wheeler's in Kennebunkport for a fund-raiser with all his Republican cronies."

I cared about fund-raisers and galas and all of that right now. No, really, I did.

"Mary Katherine—"

"All right, I'll get him."

She put me on hold and I waited for Senator Kerrigan.

He came on the line and I explained the situation. I knew I was asking for a huge favor. I also knew he was balancing the political pros and cons of granting it. The silence on the other end of the phone went on a little too long. He was going to say no.

"Listen, if this all works out, you'll be a hero. Someone who played a key role in saving people's lives in a terrorist attack. It gives you credibility when you say that the way we respond to terrorists needs to be changed. It's a cross-party issue."

Still silence. I decided to go for broke.

"It's very presidential."

He sighed, and reluctantly agreed. He said he'd place a call to the attorney general. They played golf together.

I hung up. I needed another shower. The fate of the free world was on the line and Brian Kerrigan was thinking in terms of the next move in his political career. Maybe my sister had been right about him after all.

We'll know, when we reach Fuller, if Kerrigan came through. I am not even sure we can get to Fuller if Logan is the armed camp I think it is. It would not surprise me to see tanks are at the gate.

About the only good things that this kind of firepower and government bureaucracy brings are communications. While I'll bet that the transformer supporting the Command Center is still down, all these I-am-in-charge-type organizations like the FBI and the U.S. Army will bring enough communications equipment to talk to God. That doesn't mean they will talk to each other.

I grab my radio. "I know you hate this, but I got the lead."

"Not in that piece of shit you're driving, Gibson," Lou calls back.

He has probably got that Suburban ready to do 150 miles per hour, but I have the information to give to Major Fuller

"It ain't about rank, just about communication, Lou. You will absolutely look better in that sexy Suburban, but I belong in the lead for the following reasons: I killed more bad guys today than you; I have the babe who has also killed more bad guys than you today in the car; El Duke is next to me and he never rides second; and Fuller knows me. Can't think of any more reasons right now. I know Boston is your home but you lose."

I drive off and Lou follows.

Chris asks where I'm from. Seems an odd time for chitchat.

"Massachusetts, originally. Now I live in Scarborough, Maine."

"I have no idea why anyone would ever go to Maine."

"I just said I lived in Maine."

"Another reason to stay away."

"That was almost funny."

"No, it was actually funny."

Time to call Fuller.

"Mark? Dave here. I am trying to get to you. I have pictures of the assholes over at BU, plus cell phones and computers. Can you get me past the Fort Apache that has been set up around you?"

"I will have to drive out to meet you in order to make this happen. We are just getting all the badges set up. Meet me at the garage entrance in front of Terminal C. That is real close to the Command Center, so I won't be too far from the action but out of sight in case others get interested."

"Mark, can you tell me who the guys I'm killing are?"

"It's the Muslim Brotherhood. CIA confirmed it an hour ago."

"Things just got harder, didn't they?"

"They did, indeed. Who else is with you?"

"Lou Foserelli, Fast Eddie, Neil and the Duke plus Chris . . . two cars."

I disconnect and say to Duke and Chris, "It's the Muslim Brotherhood. Lots of money from Saudi Arabia headquarters in Egypt, leadership is shared, they are rumored to have ties to Hamas and Hezbollah also, bad dudes. Very dedicated, very deadly. The stakes are even higher than we thought."

I could feel the tension in the car. All I knew about the Muslim Brotherhood was that they had tried to kill President Wheeler forever ago. Other than that, all the information David had given me was news and didn't mean all that much to me.

David had looked doubtful when I told him Kerrigan agreed to make the call. I couldn't blame him. I wasn't sure Brian would come through.

Brian Kerrigan was not a risk-taker. He was not even a visionary. He was a decent man who wanted to be President. His whole life had been calculated move after calculated move, a slow march to the White House. He was two years away from taking a shot at that dream. Soon he would begin the two-year, billion-dollar extravaganza that is the race for the White House.

President Carson won reelection by promising we'd be tough against these guys. He promised we'd be safe.

Kerrigan was going to make similar promises, but to do that he would have to grow some balls.

I have always loved politics. Half the reason I took the job with Kerrigan was for the opportunity to run a presidential campaign. Presidential politics is the ultimate sport, a true test of who is best at the game.

Except now I was thinking that maybe it actually mattered who the candidate was and what he stood for and how much bravery he could demonstrate under fire. Maybe it wasn't a game after all.

I wonder if I am putting my neck in a noose by showing up here. I may have screwed things up taking charge like this, running around the city. I really hate doubting myself, but then again, that happens every time things are about to be taken out of my control.

I see Fuller is driving his own patrol car. Great move. We will be able to talk.

He is giving me a huge break. If he brings anyone with him, more are involved in a potential court case. It shows he still trusts me and it gives us some time to trade information without his bosses and the rest of the government listening and getting in the way.

I open the door and turn to Duke.

"You two stay put. Duke, be ready to peel out of here in case this goes bad."

I climb out and stand in the cold winter air by Mark.

"Thanks, Mark, for meeting us. Tell me how much you know about the last few hours."

"Well, Colonel, there was death and destruction in the Prudential Tunnel and again on the Mass Pike. Seven nasty characters near BU were shot. A fourteen-billion-dollar tunnel under the city of Boston we call the Big Dig is now flooded and there are the yet-unexplained deaths of nine Middle Eastern types on Storrow Drive. Then there is the slaughterhouse at the Coast Guard station in the North End. But you knew all of this, didn't you?"

"Before you arrest me, here are the cell phones and pictures I took at BU."

Fuller sighed and rubbed his face with his hand. "Can you at least tell me you know what you are doing?"

"I could tell you that, sure."

Fuller stares at me for a moment, and then at the radio in his hand. He's making a decision and I hope he's not calling in that he's arresting us.

"Colonel, take this radio, keep it on channel three. That is the FBI's command net. You freewheeling, with your team, might give us an advantage. Just try to keep the killing to a minimum. I don't need to tell you that we don't need any friendly-fire incidents. I will try to feed you what I can on the situation."

Most would have slapped the cuffs on me and made a splash or a name for themselves. Most would have cared more about the law than the man or the overall good. Mark Fuller is a good man, one of the rare breed of public servants who really cares.

"Got it. Thanks. What about the plane?" I ask.

"The bad guys, as I said, turn out to be the Muslim Brotherhood and for some unknown reason they have stopped putting a guard at the back and bottom of the plane. The Bureau's Hostage Rescue Team is getting ready to attempt a takedown."

Nice. Only thing nicer would be if me and the boys were in on that takedown, but the HRT are very good at this. Let it go, David. You are on others' time now. But me being me, I can't let it go.

"What kind of a deception plan are they using? It better be a good one. We have to get the hijackers to look the other way long enough for the HRT to get up the ass and in the plane. Whatever they are cooking better work. Only get one shot at this."

"You know it," says Fuller. "My guys are involved driving the fuel truck. The FBI negotiators convinced the bad guys that the plane needs more fuel if it is going anywhere besides its original D.C. destination. Two other cars are going to have an accident on the control road to draw attention to the left side of the plane. The negotiators are going to appear to let the plane take off. Relax. It's a good plan."

Hostage negotiations are an art form. Negotiators from the FBI usually pair up, for twenty-four-hour continuous operations. They can use up to six teams, but switching who talks to the bad guys can be tricky, so some negotiators have been know to go three days without sleep before switching.

There is usually great tension between what SWAT wants, which is a takedown of the plane, and what the negotiators want—which is for them, the negotiators, to win the day through talk. When it works, and it seems to be in the process of working here, the negotiators working with SWAT basically lie to the terrorists, getting them to believe something is happening that is not. This gives SWAT time to get into the plane.

"This is probably going to go down in the next thirty minutes, so I have to get back.

"We had to ramp up our timetable even more, thanks to you and the tall looker back there getting involved with even more of these assholes back on Route 93. The CIA thinks, and we agree, that the RV is actually a mobile command center, which is why they attempted to drive it away without putting up too much of a fight on the overpass. By the way, how are you doing?" Fuller asks.

"I am feeling okay. Thanks. Sore, but okay."

"Colonel Gibson, sir, half the Command Center wants you arrested and the other half wants to pin a medal on you. There is a small contingent discussing presenting you with a bill for damages, but I don't think they really mean it. But whatever you do from here, I don't think I can help you anymore. "

"We are at yellow," came over the FBI radio.

"Colonel, now I really have to get back, and you and this strange band of yours need to disappear for at least the remainder of this incident if not a hell of a lot longer. My guys are still in charge of the airport. I will tell them to give you some room."

Mark turns to go.

"Mark, thanks again. Before you go, what about the tanker?" I ask.

"We are getting lucky there. Somehow SEAL Team Two out of Norfolk was nearby training and is on it. We are not sure who is on that thing, but my bet is that they won't be on it for long. We've trained with SEALs in the past. There's none better at this. We caught a lucky break."

Fuller drives off and I walk back to the car.

I pull open the door and Duke gives me the evil eye, the look that says a full paragraph of Dukeisms, all directed at me for having Chris along. There is no one I'd want with me more if we need to take the situation into our own hands, but he has to get over Chris being here. She has certainly earned the right after what we have been through together. Of course, she could make it easier.

I get back in the car without a word.

I hit the button on the radio.

"Guys, we need to get away from here. I think we can get some maneuver room from Fuller's guys for a little while, at least. We need to get to a place where we can listen to the HRT take the plane."

"My bet is that the parking garage next to us will work."

"Lou, you take the lead. I bet even you can find the top floor of a parking garage."

Lou drives better than I do. I have the schools, but he has the experience. He does both drag racing and oval car racing. He loves this shit. He will love showing off in front of Neil, Duke and me, and, of course, Chris. Not to mention he will want us all to see the workmanship on the new engine and suspension in his new Chevy Suburban. But the short drive may not be quite the space he needs to show all his skills.

MARCHETTI

When this is over . . . All day I had kept thinking, When this is over, dot dot dot. I wondered if it would ever really be over. One way or the other this crisis would end, but I wasn't so sure what would happen when it did.

After 9/11, we all got on with our lives pretty quickly. Some said it was because Americans are resilient. I think it had more to do with the fact that we have short attention spans. I also don't think, for all the color-coding and terror alerts, that we really believed it would ever happen again.

Now it was happening again, and this time we probably wouldn't bounce back so quickly. It was entirely possible this time it wouldn't be a coming together that happened, but more a coming apart. The first time, we were shocked. This time, I thought instead of shocked we'd be angry.

The thought more than scared me. It terrified me, almost as much as the fact that all of this had happened in the first place.

When Americans get angry, we get dangerous. We want to blame someone and get revenge. It doesn't matter if the guy in the convenience store has lived here for one hundred years, if he matches the evil we see in our heads, we'll hate him. Given enough time and furor, we'll hurt him too, all in the name of protecting ourselves.

It was all just as scary as having people shoot at you. Being blown up or shot was just a quicker way to die. The other was slower, more painful and more insidious.

Something else was bothering me. I had this nagging feeling that we were missing something. I just couldn't figure out what it was.

"Lou? Dave," I say calmly over the radio.

"You need to trade that thing in. We are only doing eighty miles per hour right now and I could have sworn I saw a brake light back there. Bad form, old boy, bad form."

"The only brake light you've seen lately is from that gorgeous woman with you. She thinks you're an old man, Gibson, and that grampsmobile you are riding."

"Lou, that is just twisted and wrong and I will not respond to such slander and anger."

Driving at fifty miles an hour in an airport or airport parking garage would be bad enough. We are approaching twice that. My back end comes out a bit; I step on the gas and smooth it out. Nice, very nice.

We arrive without so much as a squeaky tire, and I'm surprised at how nonchalantly Chris is taking this.

We get out of the car and approach the guardrail at the top of the garage. Members of our families are in mortal, physical danger. We are in a parking garage about to listen to someone else try to save their lives on a borrowed radio. Not the way I would choose to have this happen, but it's the best we can do under the circumstances. The boys and I at least have an idea about what is going to happen. Christina only has her nerves and, God help her, us.

Neil disconnects his phone.

"Dave, just got a better look at the hard drive of the clown's computer you gave me, and got a call back from my buddy from

NSA. He confirmed it. There are a bunch of references to Maine in here. These asswipes are very interested in the Pine Tree State, for some reason."

"What would the Muslim Brotherhood want in Maine?"

"It is vacationland," Duke offers.

I look over and see Neil, Fast Eddie, and Duke rechecking their gear. "You guys really think we are going to get in this tonight? I don't think so." Three sets of middle fingers answer.

Duke says, "So, young colonel, your stuff is magic and waterproof?"

No way am I going to win this, so I check my gear and make sure everything is tied down.

"Happy now?"

I get another middle finger.

I look over at Chris. She's thinking.

"What's wrong?"

MARCHETTI

Something was really wrong, but I couldn't put it all together.

"I'm not sure."

David gave me a funny look and went back to checking his many pockets.

I had that feeling that the answer was just out of reach but all the pieces were here. The air was cold. The sky was black. I looked around at the night and the strange men who now were taking up space in my world.

"I still haven't forgiven you for that crack about Maine," David said as he finished checking his gear. "Maine has lots of great things, a lot of great places. Portland, Ogunquit, Kennebunkport . . ."

Kennebunkport. Things clicked into place.

"David, we thought the plane was a distraction for the tanker. Then the Coast Guard station and tunnels, and we didn't know what was a distraction for what. What if it *all* is a distraction? What if Boston is a distraction?"

SECTION X

A great source of calamity lies in
regret and anticipation.

—OLIVER GOLDSMITH

It takes me a moment. I turn to look at the boys: Neil is nodding, Fast Eddie spits, Lou puts his head down and shakes it slowly. Duke just stares at me. I turn back to Chris.

A plane has been hijacked, a liquid natural gas tanker is probably hijacked, thirteen good people have been massacred at the Coast Guard station, billions of dollars' worth of tunnels have been blown up. All of the professionals have been head-faked by this, while a mild-mannered political consultant put it together.

"The President," I say, "is in Maine, while amassed in Boston is the entire counterterrorism response capability of the United States."

No way any of these guys are going to take this seriously. The FBI, CIA and every other agency, probably including the Secret Service, are completely focused on what is happening here and now. It will take time to turn this massive bureaucracy in a different direction and have them start truly considering that this is all just a mere diversion for something more sinister up in Maine.

There will be meetings and opinions and some hand-wringing, probably a few opinion polls and asses to kiss. Then there will be even more meetings and a few more PowerPoint briefings. They might make a phone call, but even that will take three meetings and an okay from D.C. and probably another meeting. Eventually, just to cover their asses they might send up the HRT or others, but not nearly fast enough.

If Boston is just a diversion, bad stuff may already be going down right now in Maine. The guard standing down on the airplane doesn't make any sense—it's too easy—unless it's to get our guys to take the plane—keeping the focus here. But taking a plane happens quick, that must be why they did the tanker too—make the good guys focus on two targets at the same time. The problem with that is it takes about fifteen minutes to secure a tanker—if the SEALs are on their game and all goes well. That's not a long enough diversion to keep the FBI from Maine. No, the Brotherhood probably has something else in their back pocket: another, longer delay to create and keep the focus on the major metropolis. I don't know what they are planning, but given what they've done so far, I'm betting it will be loud and bright and deadly.

I grab Duke's arm. "We are going to need fast, and I mean airplane-fast, transport for all of us plus gear to Kennebunkport, which I guess means helos. This thing has got to be going down now. Go do what you do, and do it better and faster than you have ever done it before, because we need to be out of here in the next fifteen minutes."

"Not asking much, are you?" But Duke is already moving, with the boys right behind him.

While in Kosovo our team needed to get about three hundred refugees to a safe area, and the Serbs were trying to stop us, as only the Serbs could. They were shooting anyone in the streets—men, women, kids, it didn't matter. Duke came up with armor; I mean he convinced the French to give up armored vehicles and buses. One minute we were worried about how to get out, and the next minute we had a convoy outside ready to take us to safety. Yeah, Duke is a magic man when it comes to getting things.

The boys climb into Lou's vehicle. I think Lou is actually driving faster leaving than he did when we came in here.

I know in my gut and from experience exactly what is going down at the Command Center—lots of talk, but nothing is happening, and these guys probably won't be able to get their heads out of their asses long enough to get it done. But I owe

Mark a phone call. He has helped me out all day and has earned the benefit of the doubt. I have to at least call him with what I think is happening. I hit the speed dial on my cell.

"Mark, just listen. The Muslim Brotherhood is not in Boston just for Boston. They are in Boston for Maine. I think we have been fooled big time. This is all a diversion. Carson is at former President Wheeler's in Maine for some Republican fund-raiser. A sitting President and a former President and who knows how many other politicians and big moneymen. And now everyone is looking at Boston and not where POTUS is."

"It's . . . quite a thought," Fuller says. "Any new intel or proof?"

"It's the only way all of this fits together. Everything is so random here, so flashy and loud. They wanted every bit of counterterrorism intel and manpower looking at the wrong place."

"Colonel, I will try, but I don't think I can sell it. I'm not even sure I buy it. Both the FBI and Boston police now officially want you. They want your ass in custody now, and I have not even thought about you holding evidence like the computers. There are too many questions and too many bodies with your name on them, and as for you being on target, you have to admit it is a bit strange that you have been at the scene of every attack these guys have launched today. I will tell you, off the record, some think you are working for the other side, that *you* are the distraction. I suspect the CIA is fond of that theory and pushing it."

2

I could tell from David's end of the phone call that we were in trouble. I was picturing being arrested, deloused and subjected to a cavity search when he hung up.

Foreign policy is not my strongest area. I am a campaign junkie; political maneuvers are my specialty. The fact that I work for a senator whose strength is foreign policy doesn't matter at all. I hire people who know that stuff. They break it down for me and I sell it. That, right there, says a whole lot about politics.

David disconnected the phone.

"Listen, the police are looking for us and that probably won't change until they have us. The boys and I can't stand by and let this happen. We have to go and try to help. You can come, or you can stay here, but you'd have to turn yourself in."

Turning myself in wasn't looking like my favorite option, given that I was replaying group shower scenes from some almost-porno movie I had seen back in high school called *Reform School Girls*. Both options, being shot and killed or being forced to shower publicly with the girls' rugby team, seemed equally bad.

"What about the plane? Your mom?"

This whole thing started because his mother and my sister were on the hijacked plane. We had run around, had almost been killed, had killed a lot of people and now he was walking away from that. He ran his hand over his face and looked off. His eyes had a vacant look, like he was watching some kind of movie play in his head.

"As much as I hate it, my mother's fate is in somebody else's hands now. The FBI Hostage Rescue Team is skilled, good." He was trying to convince himself more than me.

I nod. "Okay. They'll do it."

"Hell, Chris, I am officially wanted. There is no way I am going to be able to get anywhere near that plane, and if I were to try, the powers that be would think I was bringing them snacks. I wouldn't be any help, and getting myself arrested won't help the President."

"I know, David. Let the FBI get our family off that plane."

"The boys and I swore in Srebrenica that we would never again stand by and watch while the government just let bad things happen. We don't have a choice. We have to go."

"I understand. I do. What do you think happens if I turn myself in?"

He looked almost pained, and I didn't know if it was because I had asked a stupid question or because the stuff that would happen to me if I were arrested was that bad.

"Chris, there are a lot of bodies out there, and you will be the first and only live suspect they will be able to get their hands on. They won't play nice. The boys and I might not make it back today. If that happens, there is just you to pin this on, and I know what you're thinking, that you didn't really do anything wrong so in the end it will all work out fine, but that's not true. If the government needs a scapegoat, if they can't get their hands on someone else, they'll use you. They'd rather have someone who looks a little more Middle Eastern and a little more dangerous, but if you're all they have, my tall friend, you will do in a pinch."

He laughed without mirth. "And with your mouth and attitude, I can't imagine things going badly."

"But I can explain . . ."

"Think back to the 'friendly' law enforcement personnel you so impressed in the terminal when this all began. They will probably enjoy pinning this on you. If they can't pin it on you, then the public starts looking for who really screwed up."

My political instincts kicked in and I saw where this was going.

"Decisions, decisions, decisions . . ." I was hearing the voice from the commercial for the Game of Life yelling at me. I needed to start acting appropriately and stop channeling TV Land's 1970s retrospective. Sarcastic and goofy was not a helpful mode right now. I had two choices, and in the understatement of the year, neither one sounded fun.

"So what's is gonna be: sex, guns and rock and roll, or prison orange and a bunkmate named Butch?"

A girl waits all her life for the perfect romantic moment. I hoped this wasn't mine.

David's cell phone rang. He answered and said, "Mark, what do we have?"

"The Secret Service is laughing its collective ass off at the Maine idea, but just in case, they made a couple calls up to Maine."

"And?"

"And there is no answer at the Wheeler compound or at the state police barracks in Saco. Under normal circumstances, this would be causing bells to go off and lend credence to your theory, except there was an ice storm in that area last night and the power is out all over southern Maine. They are sending up some guys to check it out. Colonel, they still don't really believe or trust you.

"Colonel, this doesn't change anything with regards to you. This is probably my last unofficial phone call or contact. If you don't want me visiting you in Walpole State Prison, you need to be gone. I have just been given the order to arrest you. However, I can't do that if you are not here. Colonel, don't be here."

MARCHETTI

I felt the noise before I actually saw them. Two helicopters came up over the side of the building. One slid past us and landed, coughing up all kinds of wind and noise. The door slid open and we could see Duke was inside, kind of grinning and looking a little impressed with himself. He waved us over. David ran back to his truck and pulled out his black bag and the big scary gun that I now knew was an M4, and he shoved a bunch of things in his pockets.

He came over and yelled in my ear, "Chris, hand on the hip, like before, and bend over just a little, unless you want to wind up missing things like limbs or hair."

After everything that had happened to me today—the fact that I could see a black bag and calmly think, Oh, there's his M4—my heart rate jumped as we ran crouched over under the rotor to our awaiting ride. David helped me up into the helicopter, and by the looks of things I figured there would be no beverage service on this flight.

Duke hands me a set of headphones. Military helicopters are designed to get soldiers and equipment in and out of combat zones. They do this very well but without the slightest consideration to comfort; earplugs are necessary if you ever want to hear again after you leave the machine, and headphones are necessary if you want to talk to anyone while you are on it.

"Everyone else is in the trail bird, and yes, we took all of our gear," I hear Duke in my headset.

I nod, then notice the helicopter's crew chief helping Chris get her safety harness on. The soldier has a grin on from ear to ear and is taking his time with the chest harness. We may be saving the President, but, hey, priorities. Got to love soldiers.

"Nice work with the birds, Duke. You still have the magic."

"I found these Black Hawks just sitting at the SWAT staging area. I would love to regale you with tales of how I managed to convince the pilots to help us, but truth is stranger than fiction."

"Colonel Gibson, long time, sir. Nice to see you again," comes a very familiar voice in my ear.

"Bobby Coleman, is that you?"

"None other. Haven't seen or heard from you since you saved my guys from that asshole general. I told you then that I would pay you back someday. So, Colonel, where to, sir?"

Captain Robert Arthur Coleman was a helicopter company commander in Bosnia, flying some jerk of a two-star general who stepped way over the line with one of Bob's soldiers.

Apparently one of the female soldiers looked too good to resist in her flight suit, so this jerk decided that rank had its privileges and actually grabbed her ass. At which point the soldier hauled off and kneed the general in the balls, and he then tried to bring her up on charges. I was in the wrong place at the wrong time and happened to see the whole thing. I simply stood up for the crewmember, another in a long line of brilliant career moves. Captain Coleman has apparently gotten out of the active military, but still flies for the National Guard.

"Bob, are you sure you want to do this? Besides breaking every rule in the book, this is going to get ugly. That's a guarantee."

"Sir, with all due respect, these are my birds, not yours. Duke told us what you were involved in and what you think is going on and we all volunteered."

I am still holding the radio Fuller gave me. Luckily, he also provided me with an earpiece, or I wouldn't be able to hear squat over the noise of the blades. I am listening to the FBI with one ear and the guys in the helo with the other.

"Coast Guard helo en route, eight from the Secret Service on board on advance to Valhalla," came into my FBI radio ear

"Bob, is *Valhalla* still the code for the Wheeler compound?" I ask.

"Yes, sir, still using that crazy name. Wheeler loves it, so they kept it."

"Thanks, my friend."

I tell those on the intercom, "Turns out the phones are down and they can't get through to anyone in Kennebunk, and the Maine State Police are out of contact too. They don't believe us, but they have to check it out anyway.

"So apparently, according to those in charge, the answer to what we think is going on in Maine is a mere eight Secret Service agents. Any questions?"

Duke mutters, "Like taking a knife to a gunfight."

He is right. I can feel my frustration growing, but I need to focus.

"I know I don't need to remind you, Bob, but these guys

took out a helo over at the Pru. From what I saw, I think it was an RPG. So we know they have RPGs and automatic weapons and enough explosives to drop at least three tunnels so far. They have been very willing to use this stuff and very accurate when they do."

"Sounds good, Colonel. Are we there yet?"

Where do we get such men? I think.

This is going to be as ugly as it can get. We are going in at night with a hot landing for sure. Hell, we will probably be shot out of the sky before we can even attempt the hot landing. Presumably, whoever's doing the planning for the Muslim Brotherhood will have a great plan in Maine, one that assumes some sort of counterterrorist response. Even with what's happening in Boston, you don't take out the state police and Secret Service around the President of the United States and think it won't be noticed. They are probably expecting Secret Service; they probably aren't expecting us. We are going into it as blind and ineffective as a one-armed blind man in an ass-kicking contest. I love my job.

Those of us who walk away will have stories to tell and sell for a long time. I'd like to think they'll also hear the thanks of a grateful nation, but that's not the point. Ah, hell, we are going to kick some serious terrorist ass, and if we could get some Bob Seger music over these headsets, it would be close to perfect.

MARCHETTI

The noise was unbelievable. I had been strapped in and felt up by some young-looking guy in a flight suit. Normally this would have pissed me off, but since I was about to die, I wasn't above one last cheap thrill. I was hurtling through outer space in what basically was a tin can, and I was decidedly unhappy. My hands hurt from gripping the bench I was sitting on.

The air was filled with testosterone and bravado. The men in the helicopter couldn't wait to get there. I was wishing I was going anywhere but. No, that wasn't true. I was happy I was not currently driving toward jail.

I closed my eyes, figuring not seeing would be better; except it wasn't. The bottom of my stomach fell to the floor every time the helicopter shifted direction even a fraction of an inch. I was going to be sick. I opened my eyes and focused on my shoe, staring at it like I was trying to light it on fire with my mind. I kept my teeth clamped together and mentally chanted, Mind over matter, mind over matter, mind over puking.

The helicopter dropped down at an alarming rate and swung to the right. I really was going to be sick.

GIBSON

"Blue is set," I hear over the FBI radio.

"Bob, can you to turn the FBI secure channel to intercom so we all can hear the plane takedown?" I ask.

He does, and the next words are heard by all of us. Duke checks Christina's headphones, and she gives him a look that says she does not need help.

"Red is set," comes another report.

"We are at Black," cracks over the radio.

"Hey, Duke, HRT is using colors . . . how cute, and they are at PNR. Let's see what is next . . ." I'm not sure I can generate more sarcasm than that without pulling a muscle.

"Your status is Green," comes a reply over the radio.

Mother, we have lost enough, Joey, then Teddy, then Dad. Not you, damn it, not you. So please, Mom, no games, just be inconspicuous. Just be normal—not pink-wearing-big-haired Marge . . . just normal.

God, just this once.

"Now we shall see," I say quietly. Now we shall see. Good luck, you bloody assholes.

MARCHETTI

New voices filled my ears as the FBI started their rescue effort. They were speaking in some sort of preschool jargon, colors and numbers and not a lot of sentences. I was going to ask about it, but, for the first time, David looked and sounded tense.

Duke touched my arm to get my attention. We had to lean in, almost touching helmets to hear one another, "You saved my friend's life today."

I just stared at him, dumbfounded. Those were more words than he had used the entire time I'd been with him. I had started to wonder if he was capable of stringing a sentence together.

"Here's what's going down."

All of a sudden this very scary man was being nice to me. He began translating and explaining. Nice made Duke even scarier.

"Blue and Red are the way they are referring to the teams. HRT, like David said, is the Hostage Rescue Team, from the FBI. He used to train those guys. PNR just means point of no return.

"The Blue and Red teams are telling the Command Center they are set and ready to go. Black here means that the teams are at the point of no return. One more move and they will be seen and put the hostages at risk; if they turn around, then the terrorists might see them. They are telling the Command Center they need the go or no go signal."

I was thinking about my sister. She was a royal pain in the ass, but somehow that didn't seem like that big of a deal.

"Your status is Green," came over the radio. I knew what it meant even before Duke said it.

"It's starting."

Every nerve in my body was on heightened alert. After a day of action, it felt odd and uncomfortable to be so helpless; to feel so powerless while sitting still and just listening.

It felt like a week when there was no noise, no movement, no nothing. Just silence. Finally, just as my head was about to explode, a voice from the radio spoke.

"Clear."

I released the breath I didn't know I had been holding.

"Just under ninety seconds. Not bad . . . a bit slow, but not bad," David said. His voice was a combination of arrogance, pride and tension.

A voice over the radio said:

"Two Tangos down, two Whiskey Whiskey, Hotels all okay."

I looked up at Duke for a translation.

"Tango means *T* and stands for 'terrorist.' Two of them are dead. Whiskey is *W* and Whiskey Whiskey means 'walking wounded,' so two of the bad guys are wounded. Hotel is *H*, 'hostages.' They are all okay."

They are all okay.

She's safe. Thank God.

"Blue is at Yellow," comes over the FBI radio.

"Guys and gals, check this out. The boys from Norfolk are about to make us proud," I say. "We just heard the FBI take the plane in Boston, and now we can listen to the SEALs take down the tanker while we take a casual helicopter ride to a presidential compound. What a way to spend Christmas vacation!"

Ranger Bob comes over the intercom and says, "We are ten minutes out from the compound."

"Roger. Thanks, Bob."

From the FBI radio we hear, "Brown is set."

"You have Green."

Duke grunted in surprise. "The frogs are fast-roping already."

"Brown is down."

"Black is down"

Then, twenty seconds later, "Wheel secured. Three Tangos down."

"Black going south."

"This is Brown. Five Charlies down. Looks like about a day."

"Black, Echo secured. Two Tangos down."

"No Charlies."

"Brown all secured."

"You got to love this shit. Though some might think we were nuts," Duke says.

"Chris, what you heard and saw is poetry in motion. The SEALs, like the Hostage Rescue Team that saved our families, practice what just happened hundreds of times a year. They are the very best in the world." My lecturing colonel tone is back.

"Wings are broken . . . I say again, wings are broken," breaks into the sequence we have been listening to.

"It's either mechanical or worse," I say into my mouthpiece. "Bob, what do you have?"

"Sir, I have the Navy on Zulu. Huge explosion is being reported. Sounds like RPGs, as many as four. It's an ambush."

"Red, Red, you are at Red"—rising alarm in the voice.

"They are aborting the takedown on the boat," Duke says to Christina.

"Hope it's soon enough," I say, but I don't think so.

"Lady down, lady down . . ."

"Goddamn it," Lou says tightly.

"This can't be happening," Neil says in honest disbelief.

"*Lady down* are the code words for a sinking or blown-up ship." Duke looks at Christina, but I can see his jaw clenching.

"First they took out the helo, then blew the boat, is my guess," I say. "Bob, what do you think?"

"I think we just lost a SEAL platoon in Boston Harbor. This is your mission, Colonel. I am just the taxi. Your call, sir."

Over thirty of this nation's best are gone. I want to swear, to rant and especially to shoot. I would love time for a there-but-for-the-grace-of-God moment, but people are looking to me to make a hard, quick decision. Lives of friends and possibly a world leader are the stakes.

"Bob, we are still doing our thing; in fact, we need to invent a new speed called GetThereNow."

"Colonel, a Major Fuller is on the intercom," says Captain Coleman.

"Did we lose the SEALs?" I ask.

"Tanker is burning; helos were downed by multiple RPGs and then a major explosion. If that thing had been two miles closer, we would have lost most of the Boston waterfront. We have boats in the water, but so far no survivors. Colonel, your mother and Ms. Marchetti's sister are safe."

Mom is safe. Thank God.

"Colonel, why am I talking to you on an intercom in a Black Hawk helicopter, a helicopter much like the ones that used to be sitting here at Logan?"

"Mark, you are clearly imagining things and I worry for you, but when you get a moment, you might want to consider sending what can be spared up toward Kennebunkport, just for shits and grins."

"Colonel, what are you talking about? You know what is going on down here. I can't be expected—"

"Mark, do the right thing here. You always have." I cut the connection.

MARCHETTI

Holy Mary, Mother of God, I didn't know whether I should jump up and down because my sister was safe or if I should cry for the SEAL team—the SEAL team that was in harm's way because of phone calls I had personally made and been proud of. It had taken me a few seconds longer than everyone else to translate what I'd heard over my headset into English, but the tone of voice of the guys on the radio pretty much drew the picture for my brain. Things were blowing up, people were dying and I was listening.

My brain said, Roll film, and the images of flag-draped coffins, honor guards and riderless horses played in my head. I was back in Arlington, Virginia, in 1994 at a funeral. The sound of the guns roared and taps played somewhere.

The sky had been the most amazing blue that day and the grass in Arlington was, as it is always, a green like someone colored it with a crayon. The coffin was polished and gleaming and the flag was handed over to the weeping mother, and I stood there, my rose in hand, laid it on the coffin and then it was over; life moved on.

I knew that scene would play out for countless families and girl-friends in the weeks to come, and probably more in the months to come, after we sent soldiers to die in whatever country we decided to take over in retaliation for this mess. Except I had heard that Arlington was almost full and that it took something like an act of Congress to get buried there now. Matt had died and been buried in Arlington in 1994. How many wars and dead nineteen-year-olds does it take to fill a National Cemetery? We'd probably know soon enough.

My moment of reflection was cut short by the helicopter dipping down and my stomach rising up.

Coleman tells his other bird to step on it. With any luck, we will be able to cover the eighty miles in just under twenty minutes. Turns out we are about five minutes behind the Secret Service guys in the Coast Guard helo and gaining, or so says the radar in the Black Hawk. We can see its taillights off in the distance, which is a big no-no, since they don't know what they are flying into.

I remind Captain Bob that we should be flying in blackout mode. It's a little dangerous, flying with just night-vision goggles, but necessary if you don't want the bad guys to see you coming.

"What was I thinking? Let me turn off the . . . Oh, my, we are already in a tactical mode."

"Point taken. You fly. I will enjoy the ride." He is right. I was being a pain in the ass.

Unfortunately, the pilot of the Coast Guard helo lacked both Bob's experience and Bob's pain in the ass. He is not thinking the same way and in fifteen minutes it would cost dearly.

In my headset I hear Bob and the crew chief yell, "Missile, missile, SA-7s," as the anti-missile radar on their console rings and flashes all at once. The Coast Guard helo had been hit dead center on the left side as it passed over the dock of the Wheeler compound. It goes down in three burning parts into the very cold Atlantic. Water temperature is about forty degrees, which means anyone who survives the crash has very little time before the cold overcomes them.

We dive to the left and all hold on. Lou, Neil and Fast Eddie are in the second helo; they dive to the right. We dive for the water at about two hundred miles per hour and I can see Lou's bird off to our left, slightly closer to the shore. We go farther out to the ocean, to avoid being hit. I swear we are almost under the water. Jesus, this kid can fly.

We bank to the right and head back toward the compound. We are here to rescue the President, after all, not run from rockets. We come in skimming the waves, pop up over the dock and are just over the main house when Lou's bird takes two rounds in the tail. The tail rotor breaks off, with the blades splashing the water like a small hurricane; the body of the Black Hawk stays intact, but the top rotor blade breaks in two about twenty-five yards from the dock.

"Lou? Lou? Dave," I send over the radio. No response.

SECTION XI

I think I'll dismember the world
and then I'll dance in the wreckage.

—Neil Gaiman, *The Sandman:*
Preludes and Nocturnes

MARCHETTI

It could be a fireball, it could be breaking in two, but it suddenly seemed to me that helicopters weren't especially safe. My panic climbed. I pulled at the harness because we needed to do something. It took way too long for my brain to get that we were in a helicopter and there wasn't anything we could do.

The guys in the helicopter weren't joking anymore, but they were icy calm. The pilot did his thing, David called into the radio, Duke didn't blink.

When I was working in Pennsylvania I went on a date to the Philadelphia Zoo. We stood for a long time in front of the tiger habitat that was surrounded by a moat. A mother duck had made her home inside the moat and when the ducklings arrived they couldn't fly or climb out. They swam back and forth and the tigers decided they would make a good snack.

The tigers climbed into the water and hunted the ducklings. Five ounces of duckling were hardly worth the effort, but the tigers were inexorable. Seven hundred pounds of giant cat trailing behind a panicking mother duck and one by one swallowing the ducklings. I kept yelling at my date to do something. I didn't know what I expected, and I knew what I was saying was insane—and if I didn't, the look on his face was enough to make me see it—but I had this restless, itchy feeling that we had to do something. I had the same feeling now.

I tried to absorb the calm. Then I tried to fake it. Tried to act like they were, do the right thing, pull my weight—whatever—but there were things crawling around in my stomach and if I was passing for matter-of-fact, I deserved an Oscar. Not sure when I began to think that this whole thing was about me, but I needed to stop and climb back on board the reality train.

The helicopter skimmed the wave tops which should have scared me but I was too busy being scared by other things. The Wheeler compound sprawled along the rocky Maine coast. Ten acres of floodlit walking paths, cottages orbiting a large main house at the head of a winding gravel driveway. Would have been idyllic in a billionaire sort of way, except I couldn't shake the feeling that somewhere down there was a seven-hundred-pound cat waiting for us..

GIBSON

Bob has expertly flown us low—wave-hugging low—then popped up over the four-foot seawall. As we come over the wall, I catch a glimpse through the door and windows of the main house. Flashes of fire coming from weapons, cars in flames—we are in a combat zone. Can't see much more, as the bird is flying lower than the top of the roof of the three-story main house, but what I see tells a good-news, bad-news story.

Good news is we got here. Good news is that the fight is still going on, which means the Brotherhood has not been totally successful, not yet. Good news again, the Secret Service is putting up a hell of a fight. Bad news is we lost Neil, Fast Eddie and Lou plus the Black Hawk crew. Bad news is we are about to set down in hell.

I say, "Bob, yellow smoke for PZ."

"Wilco."

Translation: I said, *I will throw a yellow smoke canister to mark where I want to be picked up,* and Bob said, *Yes, sir, will do.*

I look over at Chris: she is holding on for dear life and has gone from white to green. It's too late to leave her in Boston, so I think it through. I could leave her on the helo, but we just lost two, and since I know Bob will go and look for survivors, it's probably more dangerous in here than it is on the ground. If I take her with us, at least she has a chance. When all options suck, you take the one that sucks the least.

Bob Coleman expertly maneuvers our helo onto the back lawn of the Wheeler compound and it's time to make a decision.

I hit Chris's chest harness release, take her headset off, grab her left hand and put it on my hip. Both of us jump out of the helo. Duke, who is on the left side, does the same. We all kneel down and wait for the Black Hawk to take back off. As the helo lifts into the air, I wish Bob luck.

"What about Lou?" Christina says urgently.

I shake my head and turn to Duke.

She grabs my shoulder. "What about Fast Eddie? Neil?"

I shake my head, then just stare at her. She knows the answer. I just have to let her admit to herself that she does. Her face crumples. I nod and then turn to Duke.

Duke uses his right hand, as he keeps his M4 in his left, and points to himself, then to the left side of the house. He then points to me and to the opposite side of the back of the house, telling me he is moving to our left, going to the edge of the back of the main house and that I should go the other way. His night goggles are down on his face, his M4 tight in his shoulder, out in front. He aims his weapon where his eyes go, first to the windows and doors as he passes them, then directly at the corner. He kneels, then lies prone and takes up temporary residence.

I give a thumbs-up to signal that I understand, and pull my night goggles down on my face. I look back at Chris. She still has her hand on my hip. On her face, determination and fear are fighting for control. I put my M4 up and check the windows and door on the right side of the house. We move.

As we come up on the corner, a large black-clad man is moving, or rather is blown backward. The back of his jacket has secret service written on it. Son of a bitch! I see two rounds exit the back of his neck and he falls, no more than two feet from us. He has night-vision goggles on and a black watch cap, can't see his face.

I check the Secret Service guy for a pulse. There isn't one. I get his goggles off and take a closer look at him. He has crooked teeth, bad hair, a dark complexion and is definitely

Middle Eastern. Of course, the Secret Service could have Middle Eastern types, in fact that would be great, considering our enemies, but there is something wrong with this picture. I make a quick check of his gear: His vest says SECRET SERVICE, but it is wrong, too thin. He does not have a first-aid kit on, which is standard for all Secret Service gear, and his sidearm is a nickel-plated Taurus 9mm piece of crap. He has no ID, no grenades. This guy is not Secret Service.

Good God, is there anything they didn't think of? Wearing the uniforms of the good guys is brilliant and has just made this already impossible rescue . . . what comes after impossible? We are in a firefight at night and now the good guys and bad guys are indistinguishable. We can see almost nothing and we can't trust what little we can see.

I take his goggles, his shiny—but not very effective—handgun and his two extra clips of ammo. I motion for Chris to take them and she does. I move to the edge of the house and carefully look around the corner.

Two, no, three cars, blown up and on fire. I count seven guys in black outfits with SECRET SERVICE written on their backs in large white letters and two other guys in suits, using the cars for cover. They are shooting at the front of the house. Also, there is firing directed at the burning cars coming from a small knoll. The Secret Service guys around the cars are in serious trouble. If they are, in fact, Secret Service guys.

From behind I hear firing and turn to see Mr. Duke Dewey taking care of his violent business with precision. He is firing in two-round bursts. I hear muffled screams after he shoots. Duke shoots, someone dies. Duke shoots, someone dies.

I pull back around the corner, face Chris and say, "Lots of trouble out there. Put on your goggles, and this gun is loaded and off safe. Just point and shoot if you have to, but only if you have to. We need to get over to where Duke is."

Panic. That was all I was feeling. Complete and total panic. My ears were filled with the sounds of gunshots and screams and whispered directions from David. But louder than all of it was a sound like the roar of the ocean. White noise was filling my head. I tried to focus.

I had the goggles on and the gun from the dead Secret Service agent was in my hand. David moved in front of me and toward Duke. I kept my hand on his hip and followed, concentrating on making my feet move, one in front of the other. Suddenly David turned and shoved me into the wall, brought his gun up and fired twice. A second guy had come around the corner. I don't know how David knew, but he did and he fired. One bullet hit the man in the chest and the other hit his stomach. Even after all that, he kept coming toward us. He was two feet away from me when David fired again. The man's head exploded and pieces of brains and skull and other parts of him landed on me and in my hair.

The white noise roared through my head. Next thing I knew, I was running.

When my mother was seven years old, she reached over a lit candle and accidentally set her nightgown on fire. She used to tell me the story about how, instead of trying to put out the fire, she ran and hid behind the refrigerator, trying to get away from herself. It never made any sense to me until now. I was running blindly just trying to get away.

I could hear more gunfire and couldn't really tell where it was coming from, but I steered myself in the direction I thought was the safest—toward the water. I was almost at the seawall when I was tackled from behind. I knew it was David, but didn't care.

"No. Get away from me," I hissed. I was still fighting him, but it was pointless, he was way too strong. He was also probably about half a second away from knocking me cold and leaving me there.

"Chris." His voice was low but forceful, and I looked at him even though I didn't want to.

"I know. I really do know. It's all right."

The noise in my head was subsiding. I really wanted to believe him: that it was all right, that we'd be okay.

"We have to do this. It's not right, and it's my fault and you shouldn't be here, but you are and there isn't any way out of this except the hard way. I need you to come with me and do what I tell you."

I had my breathing under control again. I knew he was right. What was I going to do, swim to Boston? My only option was to trust Colonel David Gibson. Amazingly enough, I already did.

The air is cold and sharp and I feel it bite pleasantly in my lungs with each breath. The manicured but brown and frosted lawn crunches underfoot. With the ocean rhythmically beating behind me, I can hear the sound of gunfire echoing all around me.

Actually, I can't believe she has not run long before this; lots of guys would have. I have seen them—run or simply give up. Can't blame her, not for a moment, but now is not the time. I need her to hold it together for just a little longer. I grab her by the elbow and guide her up.

"Right now you have to hold on, this is going to get a lot worse before it gets better."

She nods.

Duke approaches, his back toward us, his gun and eyes never leaving the corner he has just abandoned. I return my eyes and weapon to the right side. I feel Chris put her hand on my hip.

Duke fires and drops someone coming from his side. I hit two coming around the right. They have found us. We can't go to the ocean, the seawall won't help us; it would just leave us trapped. Got to attack and hope it throws them off.

"Duke, grenades," I yell as I toss two at the right side of the house. Four or five black figures round the corner, get caught in the blast and disintegrate. I grab Chris's hand and move toward the back door of the house.

"Inside now," growls Duke as he throws his grenades toward the left. Three more men coming from his side disappear in a flash of light. Duke runs at the rear door of the house shooting at the hinges and literally kicks the door in. Duke never did like doors.

I followed David and Duke through the back door into the kitchen.
It was all shiny stainless steel and natural wood and looked like a
layout for *House Beautiful*. The contrast with where we just had
been was startling.

I had taken my hand off of David's hip so that I could hold the
gun he had given me with two hands. Both David and Duke had
their scary guns up, pointing in the direction they were looking. I
had mine pointed down, just in case large bad men tried to hide
from us by pretending to be floorboards. I tried to hold the handgun
up like the sexy detectives in countless cops shows on TV, but I realized I didn't want to accidentally shoot David or Duke. I was better
off pointing down and shooting my own toes off.

I looked over my shoulder and saw six or seven men coming up
the back lawn. David grabbed me by the wrist and propelled me,
almost without my touching the floor, down the hall. I wasn't sure
how many rooms we passed, but there was a metal pinging sound
and as he pushed me down he was yelling about a grenade.

6

GIBSON

No fireball—this is not TV—but a nasty, quick, powerful *crack* comes from about fifteen feet behind us, followed by broken glass sounds. I am up, grab Chris and I step/run over her, following Duke. We need to get out of this hallway now. It's too narrow.

"Right," yells Duke as I come behind with Chris attached.

I break to my left, into what looks like a large living room. There is a big picture window, large overstuffed leather chairs, the works. Duke was telling me where he was going. He had two choices entering the room and he was letting me know which one he was taking so we did not both wind up in the same spot. Now we can cover the entrance better.

I push Chris down behind the couch that sits kitty-corner to the doorway. "Stay low," I tell her.

"Duke, next one is going back to them. They are using those Russian pieces of shit with the six-second delay, I think." At least I hope it has a six-second delay, or the only thing left of me will be pieces with holes in them.

The next grenade bounces off the floor and lands on the couch Chris is hiding behind. I am at the corner of the couch, grab the grenade and throw it back. It never touches the ground and explodes in the air as it enters the hallway; a few moans follow.

We can't stay in here. We have to move. We are really outnumbered.

Duke is out of his corner, moving low in front of the picture window, which is giving us a front-row seat of the fight outside. Looks like the good guys I saw earlier are no more, but there are at least ten bodies in front of them.

There are no better guys with a pistol than the United States Secret Service. But as good as they are, the number of bad guys and the firepower they came with just overwhelmed the Secret Service. Looks like they made the Brotherhood pay, though. I am sure we will find more bodies all over the place. I catch sight of a group of about four or five bad guys at the knoll. They are running toward the house.

Duke is past the window. He fires three rounds at the entrance. I have Chris up and moving and I fire off three rounds down the entrance hallway. We are moving toward another hallway, at the far end of the room. We have the back stairs and a hallway to choose from. We are taking fire from the hallway—not good; but up is not usually the best option either, since going up limits ways out of the house.

Returning fire down the hallway, Duke makes the choice for us and hits the stairs. His M4 is up and ready.

David pushed me up the stairs behind Duke. His back was almost touching mine as he climbed backward, aiming his rifle at the bottom of the staircase. All day had seemed dire, but now, here in the house, it seemed hopeless. When we passed the window in the living room I saw more of them coming this way. They were behind us in the hallway. They were out back. They were out front. They were everywhere, and there were just the three of us, and I didn't really count.

Community showers, relationships with the girls' rugby team and comfortable shoes sounded okay right about now. Actually, it didn't sound like a bad way to live at all; mostly because in that little nightmare I got to live. We hit the top of the stairs, Duke did something with his hands and David moved in front of me, then he moved in front of Duke. David pointed to Duke, then to himself, then to the door for the first room on the right, and pumped his fist up and down. If I had known we were going to mime, I would have worn my white makeup and black leotard. He moved into the room, pointed his gun at one corner, then the next, and backed out. What was left of our lives could probably be measured with a stopwatch, and I was picturing David pretending to be trapped in an invisible box.

Got to get back the initiative. We have to stop this running. We are on the defensive, and I hate being on the defensive. Duke is checking a room just ahead. I yell, "Need a minute here."

I move back to the top of the stairs and lie down, low profile to anyone coming up the stairs, roll on my back and pull a grenade and some wire from my vest. There is a pin holding the release handle on the M9 antipersonnel grenade. I first wrap the elastic band just once around the release handle and then pull the pin. The handle strains against the rubber band. I attach the wire to the handle and gently unroll the wire across the top of the stairs, with only enough tension to bring the wire off the floor no more than four inches. I take out my Spyderco, stick it low in the hallway and attach the wire to it. Low lighting makes this trap possible. The next dipstick chasing us will come up this stairs, hit that wire and fall down dead. Or he will see the wire and stop. It will make him think, slow him down. Trip wires work on you that way.

I low-crawl back from the lip of the stairway, get up and move back to Duke and Chris.

"That may slow them down a bit," I say to Duke.

Chris is behind Duke. When I'm back, he immediately moves forward, checking the remaining three rooms. First two doors open to bedrooms and take no more than one minute.

As Duke comes out of the second room and moves toward

the third door, we are greeted with flying wood chips and a hail of bullets. He backs away and fires at the door.

From behind us and around the corner a grenade goes off, probably mine, and then a storm of bullets start coming from that direction.

A second stairway means we have them coming at us from two directions. I have 120 rounds left for my M4 in four thirty-round magazines, plus almost a hundred rounds for my SIG and one antipersonnel grenade. Duke would have about the same.

A grenade from each end of the hallway comes flying in our direction. I shove Chris and yell, "Grenade," as I close the door to the room.

9

Almost immediately after David tossed me through yet another door-way, there was an explosion and the door blew off its hinges. I scrambled backward. David pointed to a chair in the corner and motioned for me to get behind it. So much for brave, competent and useful. I was spending all my time hiding behind furniture, and that was fine by me.

Duke and David were up and shooting toward the doorway. They reached it at the same time. David shot to the left, Duke to the right, but the bad men kept coming.

We were all going to die. It was only a question of when.

GIBSON

I have the left side of the door. I am lying down, shooting back the way we came; Duke is kneeling and firing at the staircase at the other end of the hall. We are barely holding our own. Damn, but these clowns are pissed and really pressing in on us. If these guys were stupid, they would come at us one at a time down the hall and we could kill them in the same order. Unfortunately, these are not stupid men. They are using grenades to back us into a room and they are gaining ground. I am not real sure how many more assaults we can take; I suspect the answer is none.

Duke and I are pretty good, maybe better than most in a gunfight, but with these narrow spaces and the firepower these guys have . . . well, we gave it one hell of a run. There is, as they say, a time and a place for all things.

From Duke's side the firing increases. The ceiling looks like a beehive. I can hear screams and moans. There is a precision to some of the fire, *whack*, *whack*, almost a rhythm then I hear, *"Clear,"* but it is said with an Italian Boston accent.

They are coming up Duke's side and he sees them first, but then, out of the corner of my eye, I catch sight of Neil, Fast Eddie and Lou striding into the hallway. Their weapons are singing, they are dripping wet and steam is rising off of them. In all my life, it is the most beautiful sight I have ever seen. Lou winks and says, "Take the back, we will push them to you."

I grab Chris and steer her behind me; she puts her hand on my hip. Duke is up moving to his right and down the stairs. Chris and I follow. At the bottom we file into an alcove next to the kitchen and follow the noise.

We change magazines and move toward the living room and hallway from where we started. Four bloody, deadly Arab men in Secret Service garb greet us. I shove Chris down, drop to my right knee, notice Duke doing the left knee and together we cut down these assholes. The first two fall almost together, as my bullets go through the first man and into the second, too much velocity at this distance. Duke shoots the third man twice in the head, stands up, moves forward with blinding Duke-like speed and puts the muzzle of his M4 in the chest of about-to-be dead man number four and pulls the trigger once. The 5.56 round goes through the chest, hits a bone and actually comes out and hits the floor. Bullets will do weird things sometimes.

We both yell, *"Clear."*

Almost in harmony, we hear the other boys yell, *"Clear,"* from no more than thirty feet away.

"Lou, the hallway to your front. We took some fire from there earlier," I yell.

"On it."

Duke and I scan the area outside the picture window. Nothing is moving.

From down the hallway there is one explosion, then *"Clear"* comes down the hallway, followed by the very welcome sight of the three amigos.

"Bad time of the year for a swim up here, boys," I say to what thirty minutes ago I thought were three dead friends.

"The helo passenger compartment went in the ocean intact and landed about twenty feet from the boat dock. Windows were blown out. I saw the crew get out, but two of them are hurt bad. Tide was coming in, so we made it in easy. Caught three of the clowns wearing Secret Service uniforms at the dock by surprise," says Lou.

"How did you figure out they were fake?" I ask.

"Well, all three yelling in Arabic was part of it. One having an expended RPG on his arm was another," Lou says with his wiseass tone that right now sounds so sweet.

"Yup, two good reasons there." I smile.

MARCHETTI

I wanted to throw my arms around the three guys I had seen die only a little while ago, but I didn't, since the whole group of them seemed to be downplaying the helicopter falling out of the sky. From now on, I would never say how unrealistic soap operas were when they brought a character back from the dead. Apparently it happened on a regular basis.

Since there was a lull in the action, I was ready to make a run for it. I had visions of us walking off the compound and hitchhiking back to Boston. Even after all that had gone on today, I heard my mother warn against hitchhiking. I quietly told the voice to shut up.

The boys were all standing around trying to figure out what next. I knew what next. They had come here to rescue the President and to kill bad guys. The way I had it figured, since we didn't have Carson and they weren't going to be satisfied until every bad guy was dead, they weren't done.

"We surprised them for sure," says Duke.

Lou nods. "They had a good plan and we just messed it up. They planned on the Secret Service and some locals."

"My bet is that they were almost finished here," Duke says softly, still looking around constantly.

"They have either already killed Carson and the Wheelers, kidnapped them or they were close to it. Our showing up has put them off their timetable," I say.

"Who cares? We need to kill them all," chimes in Fast. "They shot a helo out from underneath me and made me take a swim in the cold-ass Atlantic Ocean in December."

"Look, guys and gals, we need to move. We have clearly lost the element of surprise, and from the look outside, the Brotherhood is winning the war here. We need to change the momentum in favor of the good guys. I don't see anyone around here but us that fits that description. And we really need to find the President."

"Unless anyone has a better idea, I think we start by taking out whoever is shooting from that knoll out front," suggests Duke.

I nod. "Right, we find whatever vehicles they are planning to use to get away in. They can't be far. We'll go straight at them—right out the front, fire and maneuver to the knoll and be flexible after that."

I look over at Chris, who is hanging her head down and

trying to pick things out of her hair without actually having to touch it.

"Chris, you need to stay here until we clear the front lawn."

"Yup. Fine by me."

"Please don't come out until I give you the all-clear call on the radio. Then, and only then, you come directly to us."

"Uh-huh, sure."

She is not looking at me. I wonder if she is even listening.

"Do you understand? It's important. We are going from this front door to that knoll and it is not going to be pretty."

"Because what was in here was a beauty pageant."

"Chris . . ."

"No, you're right. I'm staying here until you call on the radio."

MARCHETTI

I am not usually one to give up, especially after I've committed to something in a fit of stubbornness. I usually hang in right to the bitter end, to the detriment of myself and everyone within a thirty-mile radius. Today I was going to be smart. Today I was going to admit I couldn't handle this and quit. Today I had dead guy in my hair.

I looked right at David, who seemed to be having trouble coping with my newly found cooperative nature.

"Really, I got it. Stay here. Wait for you. I got it."

We all check our weapons before moving out. We turn off all lights to avoid silhouettes and I am the first one to the door. I breathe in and slip out the doorway. Two slugs hit the door-jamb, just above my head. That was not very nice, I think, as I move to my right about three feet and go to one knee. It is an invitation to someone to shoot, and they do.

I dive to my right toward one of the burning cars, come up and aim at the muzzle flash I saw, shooting at the pinhead trying to kill me. Duke comes out the front door and moves in beside me, also goes to one knee as we were trained to do and starts putting well-aimed shots in the same direction. Lou, Neil and Fast have emerged and moved as one to our left. They are up and moving forward, firing together. It is synchronized beauty.

"Duke, I am moving," I yell.

Duke shoots cover as I move to my right along the body of the car, hugging its surface in a half crouch. I head up toward the knoll.

Lou is on the radio. "There is an access road to our left and we have spotted some interesting modes of transporta-tion."

I can see the boys moving in toward the knoll from the left. They are taking fire from what looks like two or three places.

"Duke, on me," I yell.

I fire on three of the shooters and the shooting from those positions stops. Duke moves toward me. I am moving and shooting. I take out my last grenade and flip the elastics off. I count one . . . two, and toss it toward the end of the knoll. The noise and then the screams follow.

This coordinated, improvised and synchronized assault is a dance of death. The five of us are moving to our song. We are putting out a massive amount of aimed fire, as only the best-trained operators in the world can do. The Brotherhood are killers, not soldiers; bullies, not warriors. They don't have a chance. We won't stop. We won't back down. We won't look away.

Duke moves past me, is on the knoll and kills the last man in front of him.

"Done here. You guys check out that side road and the vehicles," I say to the boys over the radio.

We did not bring an entire arms room with us, so we need to find some 5.56 for these M4s. Duke moves back toward the burned-out cars and the dead Secret Service Agents and I follow.

Duke is actually talking to, or is it at, the dead agents.

"Yours was a service without thanks. Yours was a life of meaning. Thank you, my brothers," he says as he checks for ammo.

I go about doing the same, without the chanting, but I do not comment on Duke. Duke has depths to him even his friends like me have not seen. He finds the spiritual in his bloody profession, like a samurai, a Native American warrior.

I turn toward the house and call over the radio to Chris. "Okay. Come toward the cars, straight at me."

At first I was fine with staying in the house. I tried to pick the rest of the stuff out of my hair, but it wasn't just pieces; it was sticky stuff. I wanted to do that run-away-from-myself thing again, but I clung tightly to the little control I still had.

My mother has always believed that attitude is 90 percent of life. She is the person you want with you when things go badly. She makes you fake it until you get someplace where you can fall apart. I wished she were here now, because I was half an inch away from falling apart.

Dead guy in my hair? So what? Between me and him, I was better off.

They weren't even all out the door when I could hear more gunshots. I figured people shooting at David and the boys was a bigger deal than my hair issues. The house was big and quiet and it smelled of gunpowder and death and I was alone. Before, when David and the boys had been with me, I had been afraid I was going to die. Now I was afraid I was going to die and do it alone. Somehow that seemed worse.

I moved to the window to see what was going on. I couldn't make out much, but there was a ton of shooting, and then silence. I waited for the radio to come alive and David to tell me what to do. Six and a half hours later, he finally did. Well, it could have been six and half minutes. Maybe I should buy a watch.

I peered out the door and could see him, gun up, over by the cars. I tried to walk calmly toward him, but my legs weren't listening and I came screeching to a halt in front of him, out of breath and with a stitch in my side, after a full-out sprint.

"Are you okay?" he asked.

I really needed him to stop asking that. I was breathless and borderline hysterical; okay, I was not.

"Let's get out of here. Let's just go," I said.

"We got a Bell Ranger back here and two panel trucks. Neil and Fast are rigging them now," the radio squawked in Lou's voice.

"Hold what you got. That five-passenger helo is about to go byebye. Rig it, but wait to blow it," Gibson said.

He said it with a mocking, almost joking tone. He was liking this; part of it, anyway.

"Please, let's just get out of here." I hated it, but I was begging.

"Can't do that yet." He was looking around, but not at me. "Need to finish this.

"El Duke, if it is not too much trouble, can you fall in on me? Dress it down, soldier, we have miles to go before we sleep," he whispered, totally ignoring me.

There was a large snapping sound in my brain and I literally saw red.

I got right up in his face.

I can feel her fear. We are all a little scared, but I can't let her fear distract me. I can't even afford to worry too much about her; too much depends on this and us.

"I'm not going with you."

"No, you are not," I say, agreeing with her.

That stops her for about three seconds. I have completely thrown her.

"Excuse me?"

"Bringing you here is the second stupidest thing I've ever done, second only to talking to you in the airport. At least you would have been safer in jail. We are going to stash you someplace relatively safe, and then we are going to finish this.

"My bet is that Carson is still alive. We surprised these guys in the middle of their plan. If they had killed the Carsons or even just had them secured, they wouldn't have bothered with us. They would have simply left. Not sure why else they would hang around and screw with us. They are still here. Their helicopter is still here. I will bet you all your pay that the President is still here and breathing. Not sure how much longer that will be the case, but we need to stop talking and get back to doing."

She looks at me, and I can tell she is about three million miles away from caring about any of this.

"Don't you get it? If they get out of here with Carson alive, for the next three months all you'll see on TV is video of a sitting President being tortured and humiliated. And the finale will be a public airing of the slitting of their throats or, better yet, their beheadings. If that happens, if the Muslim Brother-hood is successful tonight, our way of life will be changed for a very long time. We have a chance to stop it."

I was truly tired of David having an answer for everything. More than that, I was tired of his answers and reasons always seeming right. All this fate-of-the-free-world crap would seem ridiculous anywhere else. But when he said it, it sounded like truth, complete with a tone of duty and obligation.

In my world, I am the eldest child; my sister is the nutcase and I am the good kid. When you are the eldest and the good kid, obligation is a very serious thing. I didn't want any of this to be my obligation. I wanted to go home. But that wasn't going to happen.

A millisecond after I decided to do what I was told, David's patience ran out. He grabbed me by the shoulders so hard, I knew there would be five fingerprint-shaped bruises on each arm by morning.

"If you need another reason, these are the guys who kidnapped your sister and my mother. Cowboy up! You had your chance to sit this one out. We are moving through the woods and to that guesthouse now."

He took my hand and put it firmly on his left hip.

"Oh, and Chris? I can shoot pretty well with you on my shoulder, so don't think I won't carry you there."

GIBSON

Of all the times to get her back up, damn it! This woman has timing issues.

I refit my vest with the ammo and clips we took from the men who have died here this night. We will need this stuff a lot more than they will. Unfortunately, the fake Secret Service/Muslim Brotherhood dead guys seem only to be carrying a small amount of gear and none of it matches ours.

Duke comes up next to me. Time to go.

My M4 is up into my right shoulder, tracking with my eyes, laser on.

I call Lou over the radio.

"Blow them in five minutes. We are setting up outside and in the back of the guesthouse."

We circle left at the edge of the woods toward the guesthouse, avoiding lights, hiding in the shadows of the forest. I wonder if they can feel it. Death is coming for them, and not a glorious death. All their plans, all their hopes, will be filled with holes tonight.

We are just inside the wood line at the back of the guesthouse. Lights are on, so our NODs (Night Observation Devices) get turned off. The lawn runs right up to the woods. The woods are thankfully thick, massive pine and even larger maple, with some birch thrown in.

I stop. Thirty seconds left until it blows. Duke is to my left. I whisper in Chris's ear.

"You must stay behind this tree. Don't get up until we

come to get you. I'm not sure how many are in there, but the helicopter we are about to blow up seats five plus the pilot, the panel trucks could easily take twenty-five each."

The timing is pinpoint. The sound is beautiful. Blowing up bad guys' stuff, on time—just when we need things to happen— lets me imagine for a moment we may pull this off.

MARCHETTI

I was crouched down with David whispering in my ear when the explosion ripped through the night. I put my hands over my ears and closed my eyes. When I opened them, I was alone behind the tree.

"Cowboy up" had pissed me off enough so that I followed him into the woods. Any day now I would find a comeback line, and when I did, it would be withering.

I could hear gunfire coming from the direction of the guesthouse. I was alone again, this time in the woods in Maine in the middle of winter. Bears, wolves and possibly rabid moose were out there somewhere.

Depending on how things went inside, David or one of the guys would come and get me when they could, unless they couldn't. In that case, the next guy to come around the tree wouldn't be one of the good guys.

I wasn't a kid, I had no magic blanket, but I did have a gun. I hadn't been big on guns before this whole thing started, but now I hated them. Still, I now knew I could use one.

I held it with two hands in front of me, like all the women on TV. Thomas Magnum shot one-handed, but if Christine Cagney or Mary Beth Lacey couldn't shoot one-handed, then who was I to try?

SECTION XII

*A good plan violently executed now is better than a
perfect plan executed next week.*

—George S. Patton

GIBSON

We come out into the open as three men dressed in jeans and sweatshirts, one with a Yankees hat, come running out the back door of the guesthouse. Their AK-47s, familiar with their curved thirty-round magazines, wooden handles and folding stocks, are pointed at the ground. Pointing guns at the ground is a lack-of-training thing. It's lazy. They see us and start to bring their weapons up. The guns never make it to firing position as the men holding them are dropped to the snowy lawn.

We have about fifteen feet to cover, not too bad, actually. Duke and I move forward together. Duke fires first and three drop in the rear doorway, one on top of the other. We continue with our deadly purpose, not running, but moving faster than a walk. Weapons are deep in our shoulders. We fire two rounds each time.

I take the next two, double taps in their chests. I use my right foot, push them back out of the doorway.

I call out, "Mr. President, good guys, stay put."

I spin to my left and shoot Abdul, who has come out of a side office, in the throat twice. Duke is past me, turning to the right. He knocks one down and shoots him as he falls. I move past Duke and call out again.

"Mr. President, we are the good guys."

I throw a stun grenade into the next room, wait for the flash and bang. They make these things loud and bright, which is the point. We move in to the left. I take one guy lying down on the floor. He probably hit the floor when he saw the flashbang come in. His weapon is pointed in my direction. I shoot once . . . twice, in the center of his back.

I am hit in the left shoulder by some jerk-off who is behind a chair in the corner. I drop to one knee and shoot him twice in the chest. I get up and move across the room, weapon up. The pain is not yet registering. Body is in shock and my mind is on killing things and finding the President. The bullet hit a muscle and went through. I'll live, but it will hurt like hell later.

I move to the next bedroom. It's empty. Duke is by me, cat-like. This guy has always been able to move his 250 pounds of muscle in such a way as to create a sense of wonder in those who see him. He moves past me ghostlike, silently and with little effort.

"You okay?" he asks.

"I am for now.

"Goddamn it, Mr. President," I yell.

From the next room comes a sound I could do without. The room is a big one. Looks like a sitting room, big rug, big leather chairs and another picture window.

"He is here."

The man holding the gun to the President of the United States' head is huge, maybe six and half feet of ugly. The President is kneeling in front of him, impressively calm for having a Smith & Wesson 9mm to his temple.

"You have been very lucky so far. My brothers were weak; they failed. But I will redeem them and our cause, Allah be praised. We will—"

I have my M4 laser on Giant Arab's head. He's still talking when I look at the President. He winks. The first slug is in Giant Arab's forehead and I move forward. I shoot him twice more in the chest before he hits the floor. I drop my mag and replace it with another.

"Duke, next room."

Andrew Carson stands and looks down at his assailant. He takes the weapon from the terrorist's hands, checks the magazine and puts the gun in his waistband.

"We are on the second floor," comes the best sound I have heard in a while. It's Lou on the radio.

"Tell me you have Mrs. C."

"Nope," he comes back.

"Got it. I have POTUS." Pause a beat. "Your turn."

A silence over the radio tells me volumes. Lou is saying, *Don't screw with me now.*

"Mr. President, you have to come with me. Where is Mrs. Carson?"

"They took her outside about five minutes before you came in," he says in a voice so calm that I am taken aback until I remember this guy has seen combat. Oh, and he is POTUS. Okay, got it.

"The Wheelers?"

"They actually hadn't arrived yet. The fund-raiser is tomorrow and they were letting us have an extra day here as vacation. Very restful, I must say."

"Sir, how many were there?" I ask.

"There had to be about thirty when this started. I think more than ten took Judy out the back, toward the river."

"Sir, we are going to take you out that back door. Over there in the woods is a very brave woman, hiding behind a tree. You will please go and sit with her while we go find your wife. Sir, the boys and I have been using *Ranger* as a running password. A running password is—"

"Young man, I know what a running password is. Just go find my wife."

"Yes, sir."

"We clear on this floor? Lou, you clear yet?" I ask both Duke and Lou on the radio.

"Yup," says Duke.

I hear a flashbang, some gunfire and then quiet. The radio squawks.

"We are now," comes Lou from the second floor.

MARCHETTI

I had been crouched down behind the tree listening to explosions and gunfire for what seemed like a week. I still had the gun in my hands. My fingers were cold, my toes were cold, my ears were on fire and the muscles in my legs were cramped from staying in the same position too long. There wasn't a lot of snow, but there was enough, so I wasn't going to sit in it. If they didn't come back for me and I had to wait for someone else to come and help me, it could be a very long night. I didn't need a frostbitten ass.

The gunfire stopped and it got quiet. I waited but didn't hear anyone. I shifted my weight and peered around the tree to look at the house. Another burst of gunfire came from the second floor and I ducked back behind the tree, heart pounding. I waited but heard nothing else.

In the movies the girl always heads into the house to find the people she came with. Well, I knew how those movies ended, and since I was hoping for a different outcome, I decided to head to the main road, walk to the closest place with a phone and call a cab. Every other time David had told me to stay put he had said that if he didn't come back I should go get help. I decided to try following directions. They weren't his most recent directions, but, hey, better late than never.

GIBSON

3

Lou, Fast and Neil are coming down the stairs. I hear magazines hitting the stairs, bolts to the boys' M4s going forward and sounds of "You guys okay?" from all three. We all look at each other and nod. Neil gives a thumbs-up. Fast just stares, his jaw set. Duke makes the sign of the cross. My shoulder is starting to hurt. I take a first-aid kit from my vest and have Neil wrap it up; no one better than a Special Forces medic.

The President saw ten men take Mrs. Carson out the back toward the Kennebunk River. The Wheelers have a private boat dock and it looks like the Brotherhood has another way out, seeing how we fucked up their first plan.

Duke says to Lou, "What the hell are we doing standing around with our dicks in our hands?"

Lou looks over and offers, "Sorry, Mr. President."

I turn to Carson.

"We don't have an accurate count yet on all the bad guys. It's dark, the Secret Service and the rest of the government are still in Boston, but with the phone call I am about to make they will be here soon. For your wife's sake, though, we really can't wait."

I take out my cell phone and speed-dial Mark Fuller.

"Mark, Dave Gibson, we got POTUS. War zone up here. Mrs. C. is still in trouble. We are going to get her. The Coast Guard chopper went down about a quarter mile from the compound. We don't know how many survived. If you have a moment, you might want to inform the FBI and Secret Service that the President is in need of a little bit of assistance. No time to chat."

I disconnect.

We move, surrounding the President, and start out the door. Fast Eddie at the front, Lou at the back, I am on the right, Duke to the left, Neil near me, the President in the middle; we are all looking at clock locations coinciding with where we are in the formation. We move out the door and toward the wood line.

4

MARCHETTI

Find the road. Okay. How did I do that? My brain felt as cold and sluggish as the rest of me. I wanted to be able to keep the guesthouse in sight, since I knew there were a hundred bad guys in there. I didn't want them sneaking up on me. This meant I had to move backward. Okay—backward. How in God's name was I supposed to do that?

Now, I just had to turn around without leaving the cover of the tree. Then I'd be looking at the house and could see if guys with guns were coming to kill me. I thanked God for my metabolism and the fact that I hadn't had dinner. One more pound on my frame and I would have been wider than the tree. I slowly turned, making sure my body stayed hidden. I did it. Good. Great. Now I was facing the tree. Trouble was, I was staring directly at the tree, so all I could see was bark. In order to see the guesthouse I was going to have to take the chance that they would see me. I quietly thunked my forehead against the trunk and tried to gather my courage to peek around it.

I blew out the breath I had been holding and was about to move when I heard footsteps crunching snow. I held my breath again, and now I could hear them coming across the lawn. Toward me.

My mind was a whirl of color and panic, but no thought came. There were no flashing neon signs, no wiseass remarks, no ideas on what I should do. Actually, I did know what to do. I wrapped my hands tighter around the gun David had given me and waited.

5

"We need to get the President settled with Chris," I think out loud.

"Who's protecting who?" Lou asks.

I look at Carson, who's probably not used to being discussed like he's not actually here.

"They will protect our rear while we go get his wife."

We are almost where Chris should be hiding when a round flies past my right ear. I drop to one knee. The boys crouch with their weapons up and ready, but like me they suspect that this shot was not as menacing as the others. That was nine-mil handgun and only one shot; the assholes have all been using long guns.

I yell, "It's a misfire. I got it."

I hear a soft but heartfelt "Shit" from behind the tree.

"Maybe when I said shoot the bad guys I should have been more specific." She comes out from behind the tree slowly.

"It's okay, Chris, just lower the weapon, please."

Her eyes are huge, she is a little shaky and then she drops the gun when she sees me and just sits down, or rather collapses. I don't blame her; that was a little close even for my comfort.

"That is what I get for not calling you over the radio. Or have I finally pissed you off enough that you are now trying to kill me?"

She doesn't appear to be in a joking mood, so I make the introductions.

"Chris, Mr. Andrew Carson. Mr. President, Chris Marchetti. You two are going to stay put, please. Chris, that cottage is full of dead men, but it is warmer in there than it is out here, if you two want to move inside. Try to maintain your unusually cooperative role for just a little longer. Mr. President, I really need for you to do the same, sir."

I take off my bulletproof vest and hand it to the President. He puts it on.

"Mr. President, how far to the boat dock?" I ask.

"Less than a football field length from here. I'll show you," he answers.

"Ah, that's not the best idea we could have here today. You really need to stay put with Chris here. Consider it covering our back," I respond.

"Lou, you guys swing right, we will take the middle."

Duke and I start to move deeper into the woods.

MARCHETTI

I hadn't shot at David. He just happened to be standing in the area where the bullet went, but I was certain when he told this story he would say I had almost killed him. When I told this story, I would focus on the fact that I was now huddled in the woods with the President of the United States of America.

The President had a gun and he looked a hell of a lot more comfortable with it than I was with mine. His eyes moved over the woods. I didn't know what to say to him or what to do. I hadn't voted for him, but he probably didn't know that. Most people who meet Presidents do so at the White House, decked out in ball gowns and tuxes. They had strange exotic dinners. I had to meet a President in the woods, behind a tree, in the snow. Life can get very weird sometimes.

"Did you want to move inside, Mr. President?"

"No, and I don't intend to sit here either." Then he was gone. He crept off into the woods in the same direction David and Duke had gone.

I guess, underneath it all, the President really was just another man. Can you roll your eyes at the President?

7

GIBSON

I change my magazine, lock and load. Duke does the same. The M4s nestle back into our shoulders, NODs switched back on. We are on the hunt again.

Moving through a wooded area hunting other humans is a risky business. Doing it at night is downright suicidal. We are sacrificing our own security to move fast. We have no choice. Can't do what we need to do without taking risks. In times like these, guys like us are just expendable. Luckily, the fuckers who caused all this death are more expendable. We are just the guys to help them along.

We are not really tracking, not looking for footprints or anything else unless it is elephant-big. We are trying to get to the river before the Muslim Brotherhood can take Mrs. C. anywhere.

Duke takes the lead this time. He is better in the woods than I am. He stops, holds up a fist, points and then holds up his hand, showing five fingers. He points to his front, holds up his hand again with three fingers, then makes a zero sign. There are five targets about thirty yards to our front.

Not much time. If we go for these guys without knowing where Mrs. Carson and the rest of the bad guys are, it could go bad for us and almost certainly bad for her.

From our left we hear firing—sounds like M4s and AKs. Well, decision made. So much for seeing what we are up against before we start shooting.

I hear someone coming up from behind. I spin and see Carson.

"Mr. President, are out of your goddamn mind, sir?"

I grab him by the elbow.

"You will stay behind me. Duke is in front. In about a nanosecond we are going to be in a fight. We can't worry about your wife while worrying about you too. So please stay low and point that weapon at the bad guys. You are making my job very damn difficult."

"I'm sorry, son, but that is my wife out there. Staying behind isn't an option. Do you understand?"

"Yes, sir." I nod. "And I will do everything I can to save her. Please, just stay behind me."

Duke taps my shoulder and moves out. I get behind him but stay just off his right shoulder. Duke's weapon is covering left to his center. I have from the center and to the right. We move forward deliberately. There is firing still coming from in front of us and to the left. Rounds start going over our heads. Typical. Many shoot high at night due to unclear vision and poor training. These guys need more practice shooting at night. If we are lucky, they won't have that chance.

We don't stop. We are starting to hear voices and see green shapes ahead through the goggles. I am looking hard to the right for Lou and the boys. I see muzzle flashes about twenty-five yards away shooting in the direction of the river. All three weapons firing single shots, not bursts, controlled and deadly.

I hear some screaming. We need to get in this, help out, divert the bad guys' attention. We come to a saltwater riverbank about three feet high and see at least eight shooters. There is a forty-foot boat with a small cabin, parked, docked, perched or whatever the nautical talk is for not moving.

The President is still behind me.

"Mr. President, you have to stay here. Get down." My voice doesn't leave room for argument. I point to a spot.

"We will get your wife, sir. I promise."

I turn and move down the bank, side by side with Duke.

In my radio I say, "Ranger to your left, Ranger to your left," expecting no reply, knowing that it's a crap shoot if they hear me or not, but training becomes instinct, so I use the running password.

I waited until roughly I had my next birthday before I lost patience. My hands were frozen and could barely hold the gun anymore. I thought about tucking the thing into the back of my pants like everyone on TV did, but decided shooting myself would be embarrassing enough. If it had to happen, I didn't want to shoot myself in the ass.

I still had a nice view of the guesthouse. The lights were on, and although I knew it was full of dead, cold guys, it looked warm. Getting warm sounded really good. On top of all of that, I didn't have to walk backward to get to it.

That clinched it, guesthouse it was. I stayed behind trees until I got to the edge of the woods. Now all I had to do was get to the door. I had watched David and Duke walk straight across the clearing to the door, but they had big guns and knew how to use them. I had a little gun, frozen fingers and no clue.

In the movies when people cross a clearing they run zigzag across it. I guess it's harder to hit a moving target. It was all I had.

I took a deep breath and ran flat-out. I forgot to zig, and then I wasn't sure if I should try to zag without having zigged first. I figured if you zagged without zigging—or, alternatively, zigged without zagging—you were mostly just running diagonally and would miss wherever you were heading. While thinking about this I hit the steps and tripped up onto the porch. I jumped over the bodies in the entranceway and bent over at the waist, gasping for breath.

I heard the sounds of gunfire in the distance and moved to the back window to see what was going on. I couldn't see anything. I turned back to the entryway and looked at the bodies.

I could tell, by the trail of bodies, the gunfight had gone down the hall to the right. So I went to the left. I found the kitchen. I had the radio in one hand and the gun in the other. I put them both on the counter and took my gloves off. I wiggled my fingers. Yup. All ten were still there.

I picked up the phone and tried it. It was dead. Really didn't know why I bothered. Who was I going to call? But they always check the phone in the movies and I was grasping for anything.

More gunshots came from the direction of the water. I looked out the window over the sink and caught movement at the edge of the tree line to the right.

I backed up a little, trying to make it so I wasn't visible but so that I could still see. Two men with big guns walked out of the woods.

They were tall and had dark skin. They wore jeans and sweaters and walked as if they were unafraid, completely skipping both zigging and zagging. They probably thought there wasn't anybody up here. And there wasn't. Just me.

I ran back to the counter and picked up the gun. I looked around for a place to hide. There wasn't one. The kitchen was all modern and open-spaced and there wasn't a pantry closet. I ran back down the hallway. There were bodies everywhere. Shit! Shit! Shit! I made my way to a sitting room. It was empty except for one really big dead guy. His eyes were wide open and there was a hole in the middle of his forehead. His chest was ripped open too. Someone had made sure this guy was really dead.

The furniture in here was huge. Big leather chairs and big couch. Good for hiding behind, not as good as hiding in a closet, but it would have to do, because the room didn't have a closet and I could hear them coming.

The room had a door that led to the front lawn. Maybe, if I caught a break, these guys would head down the hall in the other direction and I could get out the door. This was almost like a plan, so I ducked down behind the couch.

I lay down flat on the floor behind the couch. I pulled the gun out of my pocket and stretched my hands out in front of me. I held my breath and wondered if seeing them coming was better than being surprised.

Soft sand with dirt, a couple of roots, but it's an easy approach. We move forward, see the Muslim Brotherhood terrorists shooting across our front to our right. They have not seen us and we are almost on them.

They are using the boat for cover, four or five of them, but there have to be others; the President said at least ten. The boat is lit up, so our goggles come off; it's easier shooting without them.

Moving with precision, we begin to accelerate. Besides saving Mrs. Carson, we have some serious payback to accomplish. The assholes are dead already, they just don't know it. Duke and I open up. I have two down. Duke kills three. The remaining three or so diehards are still shooting and their muzzle flashes are like markers, markers that we now use to kill. Lou, Neil and Fast Eddie see what we are doing and advance while firing. Now we have them in crossfire.

Duke suddenly gives me a hand signal I cannot believe. In the middle of a gunfight, he wants to take a swim or a bath. I must have read it wrong, but he repeats it. Oh, well, with Duke it's very often an ours-is-not-to-reason-why thing. I move forward. Lou and the boys do the same. We get within five feet of the dock and boat, and from out of the water three shooters come jumping up. They were hiding under the pier. Duke picks them off with casual ease and I realize again what an asset trust can be in the field.

Where is the First Lady? I shoot another one who comes up from the boat parked at the dock. I turn in frustration and realize I no longer know where Duke is either.

I could hear them in the entryway. They were speaking what I guessed was Arabic. I heard one of them laugh. All my senses were in overdrive. It sounded like they were moving the bodies around. The *thwack* sound reminded me of the guy from the van hitting the sidewalk.

Maybe they were going through the pockets like David had made me do; it didn't matter. What mattered was that they were moving toward me, not away from me, and I was hiding behind a couch.

A shadow fell across the doorway. Then one of them started talking, a stream of sounds that made no sense to me, but sounded calm and conversational. I wished I knew Arabic or that they'd speak English. I used to wish life had sound effects; now I was wishing for subtitles. The talking guy sounded like he was getting farther away from me. It sounded like he was moving back toward the front door and the kitchen. I was about to feel relieved when I remembered I had left the radio on the counter.

The voice kept on and the other guy laughed. Then the talker shouted something from down the hall and hurried footsteps made their way to just outside the sitting room. There was rapid back-and-forth between the two. It sounded like arguing. Then they walked into the sitting room.

I saw one pair of boots come into view and I don't know what happened. I just started shooting. The room erupted with bangs. I think I hit him and I don't think I was hit. I tried to get up and charge forward but I caught my foot on something and ended up stumbling backward. As I fell, I pulled the trigger and there was a bang and then a scream. It wasn't me.

I was on my back and looked over and saw the man I had just killed. Then I looked up and saw the face of a shorter, younger version of the dead man, and his gun was pointed right at me. I was totally done and I knew it. There was no way I was getting out of this.

He started to say something to me, not caring whether I could understand or not, when suddenly David's voice was in the room.

"Chris? Dave. You okay? We are almost done here. Where are you?"

My captor turned and looked behind him at the radio. I brought the gun up, and as he turned, I shot him, the bullet grazing the side of his skull. Blood went everywhere. He screamed, then I screamed. He ran out the door and my world went black.

GIBSON

Neil and Fast Eddie are checking the banks of the river and the small private boat dock. Lou and I climb into the boat, using the three steps on the side. Mrs. Carson has got to be in here, or they have taken her deeper into the woods. That way is the town and highway; no, they have to have her in here.

Two shots, both at our feet. Lou and I dive over the side and into the water. We get back on the boat on the other side, once again freezing from being in the water in the dead of winter, and are up and into the cabin. Duke was trying to get our attention and 5.56 rounds fired at your feet will definitely do that. Both our lasers land on a very broad back, and we pull off. It's Duke, and he is leaning over an alive white-haired lady. Lou moves in to help, I turn quickly with my weapon and put my laser dead in the center of the chest of a stern President.

I move aside and say, "Duke, Lou—some room for the husband, if you please, and even if you don't."

We need to check outside. The sun is coming up.

I speak into the radio. "Chris? Dave. You okay? We are almost done here. Where are you?"

Nothing.

I try again. "Chris? Dave. You okay? I thought we covered this. I call, you answer," I say again into a silent instrument.

Damn it! Not now. Be okay, please. We have been through too much. Don't let this be anything but she forgot to carry the radio with her. She has to be okay.

"Lou, I am heading back to the guesthouse. You and the boys got this end, I assume."

I am sprinting, dropping one magazine, putting in a new one. Shit! She has to be alive.

SECTION XIII

Beware the politically obsessed. They are often bright and interesting, but they have something missing in their natures; there is a hole, an empty place, and they use politics to fill it up. It leaves them somehow misshapen.

—Peggy Noonan

I came to slowly. I hadn't thought I had passed out, but there you are. There were voices off in the distance, but I couldn't make them out. For a minute I had no idea where I was. I remembered the first time I'd passed out, after doing tequila shooters in college. I'd woken up hearing a voice that said, "Pull my finger, I'm a paramedic." Well, he wasn't a paramedic and it wasn't his finger he wanted pulled. The memory alone was enough to make me struggle for consciousness.

I forced my eyes open and standing over me was someone in black body armor. He had his gun pointed at me. It was three inches from my face.

I was pretty sure Rambo here was part of the help David had mentioned. I didn't think terrorists had taken to dressing in full riot gear. Still, I hadn't come this far to be blown away by the good guys.

I did the low-growl, clenched-teeth-speak thing.

"Come here often?"

A voice I almost recognized came from somewhere else in the room.

"Glad to see you're all right, Ms. Marchetti. I have enough paperwork to fill out as it is."

I turned my head to see who it was. It was Fuller. He was grinning. Just my luck.

"You want to tell RoboCop here to back off?"

He waved the guy off and I sat up.

"Would you like to tell me what the hell is going on here?" he asked.

Gee, that was a good question. Wish I had a good answer. Flashes and pieces of the day's events swirled around, some just out of reach.

Another SWAT/Rambo clone came into the room.

"House is clear. Lots of bodies, though."

"Lots of bodies" seemed like an understatement. I stood slowly and brushed myself off. I was tired—really, really tired. After a coffee the size of a keg, I was going to tell Fuller everything. David and the boys had . . . The thought had started out being that David and the boys deserved a medal or a lynching or both, but suddenly it dawned on me that they weren't here. The blood rushed from my head and I thought I might hit the floor again.

I looked up at Fuller. "Where is David?"

2

I start yelling the running password, "Ranger," just in case Chris remembers what I told the President. I jump over the bodies in the doorway, and run into an MP5 held very steady by a very large man dressed in all black. His helmet is black. His goggles are black. His vest with nasty implements is black. His boots are black and he is yelling at me to drop my weapon.

"Fuck you! You drop your weapon," I yell. "Where is Chris Marchetti?"

I move forward, and so does the big guy. Problem is, he has friends.

"I don't know who you are and I don't care," comes another voice attached to an MP5, "but if you don't drop your weapon we are going to shoot. Your choice."

Before Fuller could answer me, the screaming started. Okay, it wasn't really screaming; it was bellowing. When people started yelling "Drop the gun," Fuller scrambled down the hall. I followed.

"Nobody shoot! Everyone put your weapons down," Fuller said authoritatively.

"He's okay," he continued, referring to me. "Colonel, when we came in here searching for the President and Mrs. Carson, this place was filled with dead Arabs and one redhead, who we thought was dead. But she let us know that she was very much alive," said Fuller, trying hard not to laugh.

I rounded the corner and saw David along with a billion guys with guns.

I wrapped my arms around myself and leaned against the doorjamb. I was trying for nonchalant. I was trying not to go to David and do that throw-myself-in-his-arms chick thing.

Bottom line, he was okay. Funny, my definition of okay didn't used to include a bullet wound in the shoulder, but things had changed.

I gave a little wave from the doorway. "Hey."

4

"Hey"? I am beat up and bleeding; light-headed from exhaustion. I am expecting to think, Thank God she is alive, when I get a wave and a "Hey." I am glad she is okay, but maybe this one is just a little too high-maintenance for me. Then again, she is a package.

The boys bring the President and the First Lady up and into the house. The place is crawling with cops in every uniform possible. The boys and girls from Langley are in plain clothes; that's a sort of uniform as well, each plain-clothed individual dressing alike. FBI and Maine State Police windbreakers are plentiful; some say crime scene or incident response team. The bottom line is there is a buttload of agents and cops all over the place, with more photos being taken than at a wedding. There are cops putting things into bags, cops taking fingerprints of dead guys, cops taking notes, cops talking on cell phones, cops using laptops, cops drinking coffee, cops doing their thing. In corners of rooms there are muffled conferences, secret talks and frowns and looks directed at us.

Fuller leaves his conversation in the corner, finds me and motions to the door.

"Colonel, care to take a walk?"

I shrug. "Okay, let's stroll."

So Mark, who is two states north of his jurisdiction, is the messenger, I figure. The Feds, especially the Secret Service and the FBI, have really got a problem on their hands with what we have done here and in Boston. This should be really interesting.

"So, Colonel, in Boston we counted over twenty members of the Muslim Brotherhood that have gone to paradise. Up here in Maine, not sure how many are yours, but around this guesthouse and down at the dock there are thirty to fifty or so very dead religious extremists. Most have two shots to the chest, very professional."

I just shrug, not sure where he is going with this just yet.

"And your friend Chris killed at least one up here, probably badly wounded another asshole that we haven't found, but will. The President is singing your praises to one and all and I heard Mrs. Carson say she was going to adopt the lot of you."

"Mark, this history lesson is very nice, but I am really tired and my arm is starting to act up, so what is the point here?" I ask.

"Funny you should ask," Mark says.

He looks a little weird, so I say, "Wait a minute, before we are all taken out back and shot, I need to get Chris and the boys out here to hear this. Also, we're going to have to account for all the Brotherhood soldiers and check the area for survivors . . ."

He stopped me, "You're not alone anymore, Colonel, We'll take care of that. Gather your team."

I move back to the guesthouse and stick my head in the door. Duke is regaling all within earshot with the story of how he saved the day. They are all listening, the SWAT guys, medics, suits from at least twelve different agencies, even the Carsons.

"Lou, Neil, Fast Eddie and Your Excellency Duke. You too, Chris. Can you all come outside for some fresh air?"

"This FBI medic just lent me his aid bag. Let me touch up that shoulder before you go any further," says Neil.

He first cleans up the wound, checks the entry and the exit, saying, "Both ends look good." Cleaning crème, three pain pills and a tetanus shot, and I am okay until I see a doctor. He takes my makeshift arm bandage and puts on a new one. We all go out front with Fuller, who is standing in his Massachusetts State Police grays-and-blues with the shiny riding boots.

"Chris, and the rest of you criminals, it seems that we have a dilemma. On the one hand, you are thugs, mercenaries, killers without any legal authority who today have killed between thirty and fifty very bad men. On the other, you have also saved the lives of thousands of citizens as well as the President of the United States."

"We went over the speed limit," Duke adds.

Now we are in real trouble. Duke is making jokes.

Fuller just smiles and looks down. "That too, but here is the thing. They don't want citizens saving the world. We can't let it be known that the full might of the United States government was once again made impotent by a small group of assholes. So what shall we do?"

We all look at each other and know what is coming. I think that Chris gets it. We're in her sphere now more than mine: politics.

I say, "Guys and doll, let me take a stab at this. How about this, Mark? We were never here or in Boston. You guys did it all."

"No interviews on Fox, no parades, no schools named after you, no state dinners, no women craving you?" Fuller asks skeptically.

Lou just smiles. Neil is nursing a beer. Fast Eddie turns to leave. Duke stops in midbreath and asks, "But the same amount of women who crave me now can still crave me, right?"

"Naturally," answers Fuller.

"I can live with that."

"So, we let the government spin this any way they wish, and in exchange we don't get arrested. Did I get that 'bout right, Mark?" I ask.

"All except the reward money."

"The Hero Program?" we say in unison—except Chris— and then Duke continues for us.

"You mean that worthless, we-offer-the-money-but-we-decide-how-much-of-it-you-get, State-Department-run deal? You actually had money on some of these guys?"

"Yes, Duke," says Mark. "About ten total."

"Typical government, ten thousand dollars for mass murderers. No wonder no one gets turned in for this bullshit," Duke bellows.

"Well, actually, it's a few more zeros. Ten million. Uncle Sam has wanted a few of these guys for a while."

We all look at each other, and I say, "So, we agree to what you suggest and the government buys us off for ten million. We walk. You guys are heroes while we go home?"

Fuller nodded. I was standing there listening to the exchange but not really believing any of it. See, the trouble with the whole I-do-politics thing is that most people who do it really believe in some-thing, maybe not the same thing but something, and they believe deeply. They pretend they do it for the rush, and that's a lot of it, but there is always the fundamental underlying stuff. They believe in truth, justice, the American way and maybe God in school or God in the bedroom or free hot lunches. Whatever it is, it usually rears its ugly head at the worst of moments, like mine was about to, right now.

"Excuse me! I'm sorry, can anyone here say 'cover-up'? Let's try 'conspiracy.' Anyone? Anyone?" I did my best impression of the teacher in *Ferris Bueller's Day Off.* They all just looked at me.

"Sorry. Generational thing. Let's try, are you *nuts?*"

I was met with blank stares.

"Let me see if I understand you correctly." I pointed to Fuller. "You want the American people to believe that the government, and all its agencies, acted appropriately? They all did their jobs and saved the day?"

He met my eyes and nodded. Incredible. I swear we never learn.

"Tell me why. Why should I go along with this? It means noth-ing changes. Ever."

"Well, first, it will keep you and your friends here out of jail."

I opened my mouth to argue, but he put up his hand.

"Ms. Marchetti, please. Under normal circumstances you would be right. We wouldn't get very far with criminal charges against you. But these aren't normal circumstances, and the federal government has obtained some very impressive powers, courtesy of the Patriot Act. We could arrest you now, and I promise you, it would take months to even begin to sort this shit out."

No one really knew where I was. If they arrested me, it might stay that way. In only a matter of hours, I could disappear into a cell.

"You don't scare me. Senator Kerrigan knows about some of it. How do you plan on getting him to fall in line?"

"Already done," came a voice from the front porch.

We all turned, and there was the President.

"We've already contacted your senator, my dear. In exchange for a few promises, your boy was more than happy to toe the line. I'm afraid he's not the man you thought he was."

Actually, Brian Kerrigan was exactly the man I thought he was. I had just hoped for better.

I looked over at David and his bleeding band of brothers. Their expressions were still blank. "Country" had been said by David more than a few times today, and he had said it with that tone you get from military guys: that reverent, willing-to-die-for-it tone. I guess I was just a little surprised that, after everything he'd been through today, he'd be willing to lie for it too.

"No," I said. The word actually surprised me. My brain sent a message to my mouth to stop, but my backbone got in the way.

"No way. No deal. Go ahead and arrest me."

6

I don't need this right now. I want to get away from here, clean our gear, take a shower, count our money—anything but stand here and argue about reality versus fantasy with a woman who is a flaming liberal, a tell-the-whole-truth-nothing-but-the-truth type. I am back to wanting to kill her.

"Mark, let me put the cuffs on her," I say.

The President waves his hand and walks down the steps.

"Ms. Marchetti, may I call you Christina?"

She nods and we all step back a pace.

"Christina, I can see why you would think this is only a conspiracy. That this is only to save our cushy jobs and make us look good."

His voice was clear and strong, but quiet. "We could tell the world exactly what happened and you will look heroic and have some time of fame and everything that comes with it. The men and women of the intelligence community will look terrible, as well as many of the men and women in the services. There will be outrage and committees called and maybe—and that's only a maybe—when the circus dies down there will be some change.

"The Muslim Brotherhood may have failed to kill me, but they will have succeeded in some ways as terrorists and our enemies around the world will be encouraged to try again and again."

His voice softens, becomes fatherly. "And you? Well, in addition to fifteen minutes of fame, you may have to disappear."

"Are you . . ." Chris looks around. "Is the President threatening me?"

"Oh, not at all. You'd be disappearing for your own good, Christina. While being hounded by the media in our country, you'd be a target for the terrorists from other countries, I'm sorry to say. The Muslim Brotherhood and every extremist out there will know you are their enemy and they will come for you. You, your family, friends, all targets.

"Christina, you may go to the press. That is your right as an American citizen, and I won't take it away, nor let anyone else do so. But I will ask you not to, and I will make you a deal. Let us control how the media and world hear about this, and you will not only go home and be rewarded, but I promise that you and all these brave men will get to testify in a secured facility to the assembled classified intelligence community about what really happened. We *will* learn from this and do better. We *will* keep the American people safer, and I truly believe that this is the best way to do that."

I remember why I voted for this man. Christina is just staring at him, thinking.

I take a step toward her. "Is there a possible compromise here, somewhere?"

I didn't vote for this man, but he was still my President. I hear politicians speak all the time, and this man was obviously a great speech-giver. I felt as though he believed what he was saying and he might even be trying to do the right thing, not just for him, but for me and the country.

I shook my head. I knew I was going to give in. I took a deep breath and thought for five seconds more. I wanted to believe I didn't have a choice, because that would make this easier, but that wasn't true. We always have a choice.

I didn't look at David. I wasn't doing this for him. I looked at President Carson.

"All right, Mr. President. We have a deal."

He smiled and shook my hand and the Secret Service escorted him back into the house.

David reached out and grabbed my arm. "You made the right call."

"For the record," I said, my voice low, "Senator Kerrigan isn't the only one who didn't turn out to be the man I thought he was."

And I walked away.

I turn to Fuller.

"You know, in a lot of ways Chris is right, but it doesn't matter."

He nods. "Colonel . . . David. I don't disagree. It feels like the corpses aren't even cold and we're all trying to cover our asses. I understand. You're not a man who trusts the people above you at all, and that's what you're being asked to do right now. A lot of mistakes were made and you are going to have to trust . . . have to have faith that there are some good people who want to fix things. Have faith in the President. Have faith in me, David. We both know what happened here and we both know it needs to be fixed. Can you do that, David? Have a little faith?"

Everyone is staring at me, except for Chris, who is heading back to the house.

"I need to get back and get my mother. "

I walked back up to the house, found a chair in a corner and folded myself into it. God, was I tired. Unfortunately, no matter how tired I was and no matter how much I didn't want to do it, there wasn't any way to put it off any longer. I borrowed a cell phone from one of the boys in black and took a deep breath. Like it or not, I was going to have to call my father.

On a good day, my father and I manage to achieve civility. On a bad day, well, let's just say it's not pretty. My father is an old-school Italian masquerading as an enlightened political science college professor.

He thinks I should get married. I think I should maybe own a houseplant first. He thinks women are good for two things. I can't cook, and although I haven't had too many complaints in the other department, I haven't had that many compliments either.

I really was not looking forward to this. At least I could tell him that Colleen was safe.

God! Colleen. I had barely thought about her in hours. Sure, there had been a few other things going on, but . . . wow . . . I choked back the tears and emotions that came from nowhere and dialed. It was some ungodly hour of the morning, so when he answered I cut right to the chase and briefly explained that Colleen had been on the plane that had been hijacked. He proceeded to yell at me.

I held the phone away from my ear.

Normally any conversation with my father follows the same script. It starts with a "Hi, baby," and rapidly moves into a list of things I've done wrong, then moves on to the ever-lengthening list of things I could have done better, and it closes with an exasperated declaration that he's not going to live forever so I'd better find a man who is willing to put up with my bullshit and pick up the tab. Then he tells me he loves me and hangs up.

Even now he was true to form. He managed to blame me for not noticing there were terrorists waiting to board the same plane as my sister, then berated me for not staying at the airport and for not calling sooner. His dismount had an added flourish because this time it was both Colleen and I who needed to find husbands. My father yelled that he was getting in the car and would meet me at the airport. Then he said he loved me and he hung up.

And he sticks the landing! I made a cheering crowd sound. I didn't realize I had said it out loud until I noticed that everyone in the room was staring at me. David was in the doorway giving me the she's-nuts look. Duke actually turned his head a fraction of an inch to look at me. He might have even raised an eyebrow.

I started laughing and couldn't stop.

I was glad my sister was safe. I really was. But if I was going to have to deal with both her and my father after this day from hell, I was going to need a beer. Six-thirty in the morning and I was thinking about beer—another item for the therapist I was going to need.

When I finally managed to stop laughing and began to focus, I got stuck on one thought. I needed to go home. I wanted my car.

Part of the charm of always being the driver is that you are almost never trapped anywhere. You get to determine when you leave. I didn't have that option now. I was trapped in Maine, yet another addition to what hell could look like.

Fuller strode in and whispered in some officious-looking guy's ear. I assumed he was relating that we had all agreed to the deal and would behave ourselves. The man smiled a smug I-knew-they-could-be-bought smile and scurried out of the room, probably to report up the chain of condescending assholes that led directly to the President.

"Major Fuller, I need to get out of here. How do I do that?" I asked. I'd be damned if I'd ask him for a ride, but I was desperate enough to take one if he offered.

Before he could answer, David spoke from the doorway. "Come on, I'll take you."

My mouth, for the first time in history, actually checked with my brain before speaking. I could take a ride from David and endure an hour of high-speed mental torture, or I could go with my first instinct and say *When pigs fly*, and wait for some random, low-ranking military or police person to be assigned to take me home.

I thought of the policemen who had wanted to search my bag at the airport; Mullins and his car; Fuller, who had dubbed me "Legs"; and the guy who'd had his gun pointed three inches from my face when I came to on the floor in the sitting room.

Better the devil you know.

"Okay, let's go."

She follows Duke and me out of the house and over to where the boys are standing.

Mrs. Carson somehow heard Chris talking about wanting to go home, then spoke to a Secret Service agent, who ran off.

She comes over and graciously thanks us and promises in a motherly tone not to worry, she won't let us be hurt. I think she means it. I tell her we need to go back to Boston; that my mom and Chris's sister had been on the plane. She smiles warmly and points to the Secret Service kid running across the lawn with a set of keys.

"Hey!" complains Duke. "I rescued her. How come you are driving her home?"

I look over at Chris. I'm not sure what the look on her face means, but I'll go with not happy.

"I promise to drive only twenty miles over the speed limit and we can stop for coffee at every McDonald's we see. Okay?"

She doesn't say anything.

"Duke, you coming?"

"Nope. I wouldn't go anywhere with you driving like that. Besides—Lou, Neil, Fast Eddie and I need to figure out how to screw you two out of the money. We have a small island in the Caribbean to buy. Always wanted one of those."

He stops, puts his head down, then looks up at Chris. He moves toward her almost like a dog who knows he has done something wrong. I can't believe it. He walks up to Chris and grabs her face in both his enormous hands and smacks a big wet one on her. He pulls back and says, "I know, I know, there is no time for us. Just wanted you to have something to remember me by." He walks away.

I am laughing. Can't stop. The man must be seeing an entire team of psychiatrists. Chris is, for the first time since we met, completely and totally speechless.

Chris and I head toward the 2008 Cadillac STS. It is not my sleek, extremely powerful and ever manly Escalade, but beggars can't be choosers.

"I'll get the door for you," I say to Chris. She gives me a steely-eyed look. I bet she's trying to decide whether to open it herself.

I open the door. She climbs in and busies herself with the seat belt.

I raise both my arms up and say, "What?" and then close her door.

The Caddy is black, of course, with only about a hundred miles on it. It is brand-new and begging to be driven, and driven well. Cadillac put a lot of time and money into this beauty, and now I am going to drive it slowly to Boston. I have hauled her beautiful ass across half of New England, explained myself in ways I never thought possible, killed to protect her, lied for her, introduced her to the boys and now I am a goddamn chauffeur. The things I do for this woman.

"Okay, here is the deal. We have about one hundred miles to go before we get to see our families. Given my current speed limit restrictions, depending on traffic and road conditions, it will take around two hours. We could play Bob Seger tapes if I can find any."

"Cars haven't played tapes in ten years."

"We can wax eloquently about the last twenty-four hours. You could profess your undying love and affection for me. Or you can get in the back, curl up in the fetal position and snore."

"Bite me."

EPILOGUE

Every saint has a past and every sinner has a future.

—OSCAR WILDE

MARCHETTI

It had taken a few months, but life had returned to almost normal. I quit my job with Kerrigan, packed my new grown-up furniture and moved back to Rhode Island. Every time I try to get out, they suck me back in.

My part of the reward money allowed me to buy a place at the beach and to survive without working. For now I decided I was done with politics. Politics requires being a grown-up, wearing big-boy pants and choosing the lesser of numerous evils. I wanted to find a cause, something I could believe in blindly.

I had told my mother about what had happened, but she was the only one, and she'd never tell. My mom was the only member of our family who could actually keep a secret, although I was learning fast.

I had seen David and the boys once since it had happened. I was coming out of the room after having given my testimony; they were waiting to go in. We hadn't spoken, just nodded recognition.

I had been having trouble sleeping. My brain wouldn't shut off and sometimes the pictures from that day replayed through my mind at random. On those nights, I sat on my porch bundled in my Irish sweater with a blanket over my legs and listened to the waves until the sun came up.

Boston was being rebuilt. A total of 189 people had died during the incident. It was significantly less than 9/11, but the American psyche had taken another blow. We were even more wary and more suspicious of Arabs and Muslims.

Within two weeks, the President announced that we had infiltrated the terrorist camp in Yemen that had housed the guys responsible for the carnage. We had killed them all. He was very public in his pronouncements that everything was under control. He had a 77 percent approval rating, and 79 percent of the American people found him trustworthy.

GIBSON

Running on the beach is fun, quiet and good for me. It's raining and snowing at the same time, a typical Maine winter day by the ocean. I am the only one on the beach, which, of course, is exactly why I am out here. Seven to ten miles today, pretty normal, and a chance to stop thinking for an hour. The air is cold, which is as it should be in March, but the black watch cap, cool-guy Oakleys, Gore-Tex running suit, Asics Gel MCs on my feet and my ignore-the-weather attitude make everything moot but finishing the run. So far, most of me feels good. I cut out and over the stairs over the seawall and head for the house. Going to have lunch with Mom today and see how she is holding up.

After the hijacking, she was a brief media star, along with every other passenger who had their fifteen minutes of fame. Mom did super until she made a pass at Bill O'Reilly. He was not amused (or interested) and made sure her TV career was over before it started.

There is a car in front of my house. I don't recognize it. My breathing slows, becomes controlled. Two men are sitting in the front. One has something on his lap. I come up on them from the back. I move along the driver's side—quick and aggressive—and pull my SIG from its holster. I open the door. I drag the driver out and to the ground. My knee is on his throat and the business end of the SIG is pointed at the passenger's head. The asshole is carrying a TV camera.

"I'm with Channel Seven News," comes a strangled voice.

The camera guy is a pro. His camera is on and aimed at me as surely as the SIG is aimed at him.

"Who are you guys?"

"Colonel Gibson, I am Mike James with Channel Seven," the driver manages as I take my knee off his chest. I motion to him to stand. As he gets up, I can see the wheels turning: he is thinking he will get an Emmy for this.

"I am working on a story that suggests that you, a woman and four other mercenaries were involved in, or played a major role in, what happened in Boston. Are you the unknown hero of the country? I wonder if you would care to comment."

"There are just so many things to say, Mike. May I call you Mike? But right now, and I always wanted to say this, no comment. Actually, there is one comment. Fuck you, Mike," I say this in my I-will-kill-you-and-enjoy-it voice. I let myself into my house and close the door on Mike and his cameraman.

I could have taken the tape, but what would be the point? They got us, or they will eventually. The camera guy is just doing his job.

I have not talked to Chris or the boys since the incident. There wasn't anything to say. Now I have a reason. She needs to know they are on to us. I can get to the boys later.

I pick up the phone and dial.

MARCHETTI

The sun was up now. The weather called for a mix of rain and snow, but spring was coming. I grabbed the blanket and my coffee and walked inside. The phone was ringing.